APRIL YATES
ASHTHORNE

Ashthorne

ISBN (e-book): 978-1-7399968-7-1

ISBN (paperback): 978-1-7399968-6-4

Cover art and photography © Donnie Kirchner

Book formatting by Claire Saag

For Vicky, always.

CHAPTER ONE

Ashthorne House had the strangest combination of desolation and grandeur Adelaide had ever encountered. The grounds on which it sat were woefully neglected. Weeds sprouted from the gaps in the stone steps, and some of the brickwork was crumbling, but everything else about the house was striking.

Even the door, which was solid oak, exquisitely carved into its namesake. A robust trunk merged into branches reaching heavenward. The negative space between the branches, filled with gold and red glass, gave the impression of an autumn sunset. The craftsman's skill was clear, as Adelaide barely saw the join connecting the two halves of the door.

Inside, the hallway took Adelaide aback. With its marble floor and grand staircase, she half expected the lady of the house to come sweeping down it, demanding to know what had brought her here.

An extraordinarily tall woman greeted her, introducing herself as McGowen, but offering no first name. She regarded Adelaide with curiosity, ushering her in without another word and not once breaking her gaze.

McGowen had the most unremarkable features Adelaide had ever seen. A complete absence of character coupled with the absence of a first name added to the notion that this was not a fully formed woman, but a cold marble blank upon which a skilled sculptor may carve. It was rare for Adelaide to feel short, having always stood a little taller than her classmates.

McGowen continued to stare down at her. Eventually Adelaide faltered and spoke.

"I am in the right place, aren't I? Ashthorne house?"

A faint cry answered, though Adelaide could not tell from where it had emanated.

"If you weren't in the right place, I'd have told you."

Against her father's will, Adelaide had joined the Voluntary Aid Detachment, received her basic first aid training from The British Royal Red Cross Society, and found herself at the newly appointed convalescent home. In her mind, she'd had no other choice but to offer her assistance, her own brother, Clark, having died in service the previous year.

His death had been the catalyst that sent her mother spiralling ever further down into her barbiturates addiction. Adelaide had grown used to occasionally finding her mother passed out on a chair. After Clark died, occasionally turned to daily, and she'd sometimes notice her father looking at her mother with such detestation that she knew he was willing her to take too much of the vile white powder one day, and never wake up from her slumber.

Adelaide wished that too sometimes. It hurt her to think like that, but every time she'd had to look into those vacant eyes, revulsion erupted from deep within her core. It wasn't fair the way she got to run away from Clark's death, while the rest of them had to feel that pain daily. It was the reason she'd had to get away; the hatred of what her mother had become, and fear that the same future awaited her.

"They've tasked us to do monumental work here," McGowen raised both hands in a grand, sweeping gesture that caused Adelaide to step back lest she be struck, "and I expect you to show proper respect to the Doctor."

Her tone held all the zealotry of religious fever that skirted along the edge of sexual.

"Of course," Adelaide said. "I've been told he is quite innovative regarding his treatments."

"The man is doing monumental work, although he's not yet aware of just how significant it is."

She gestured for Adelaide to follow.

"Gentlemen callers are strictly forbidden," McGowen said, as she led her through the house. "In fact, we discourage all dealings with the villagers."

"You'll have no trouble with me," Adelaide said.

McGowen ignored her and continued laying down the rules of house and employment. Adelaide, taking her cue from McGowen, did not hear a word, focused as she was on the house's wilting beauty. Marble hearths thick with coal dust, yet long grown cold. Conspicuous squares of vibrant colour remained on faded flocked wallpaper, its edges peeling away at the skirting.

Finally, they reached the attic room; metal bedsteads ran the length of both walls. The low light of a winter's afternoon streamed through the large porthole window overlooking the front of Ashthorne. Odours of lightly sanded wood and dust filled Adelaide's nose. It reminded her of her boarding school dormitory.

"Naturally, you will share the quarters of the household staff." All the beds were bare, save for their thin mattresses. "Not that any reside on the premises anymore."

Like most grand houses, the Great War had dealt Ashthorne a substantial blow. The combination of losing his young workforce and the loss of business had decimated Bramwell Ashthorne's livelihood. Ashthorne House had once bolstered a full roster of servants and maids. Now it had been reduced to two, a mother and daughter who lived in the village. The pair only worked Monday to Friday for a few hours a day, leaving the Ashthornes to fend entirely for themselves over the weekend.

McGowen told Adelaide this with something approaching glee, and her remissness about the Ashthorne's financial situation shocked Adelaide somewhat. There was not a hint of gratefulness for their opening their home to the cause.

"Remember, you are not in their employ. You are not to be torn from your duties by running around making tea and cleaning up after them."

"Are there many nurses here?"

"No dear, you are the only one they have graced us with thus far."

"Is that usual?" Adelaide said. An edge of nerves fringed her words.

"No."

Adelaide nodded as she stepped into the room, choosing a naked bed by the window.

"The nature of our work here deals primarily with the mind and soul. The injuries of these men are horrific, but for the most part healed. Try not to stare at them." McGowen said.

Adelaide was insulted. *What kind of woman does she take me for?*

"Of course."

"We haven't been here very long. I was blessed to have been with Doctor Roskopf at his last posting. He is an extraordinary man who deserves the utmost respect. His work will change the world."

McGowen appraised her once more before marching away.

Adelaide unpacked her meagre belongings as the weak winter light dimmed and then died.

ᚠ

Ashthorne Manor, although just as large as other residences chosen to serve as a convalescent home, was deathly quiet;

there were only four men here when the house could easily accommodate at least forty or more.

The letters Adelaide had received from friends who had enlisted described busy bustling places; days spent changing dressings, cleaning wounds, and kitchen duties.

Exhausting, hard work, but which at least offered a semblance of achievement and satisfaction.

The ward, which had been set up in Ashthorne, comprised of a ground floor room into which four hospital beds had been placed, along with a wooden desk and chair for the nurse on duty.

It was on Adelaide's second day working that she noticed the mirror hung upon the wall.

It dominated the room. Six feet wide, five feet tall, the frame an intricate carving of overlapping squares and triangles: very modern.

How on earth had they got it in the house unseen, let alone hung it on the wall? There was no way to avoid the mirror's gaze, bar flattering oneself against the wall it hung upon. Her doppelgänger stalked Adelaide, a constant companion at the edge of her peripheral vision. And sometimes, just sometimes, Adelaide didn't recognise the black shape drifting into the corner of her eye.

In her brief time there, Adelaide had spent her time mostly idle. The injuries the men had were, as McGowen had said, mostly healed. Still, she had to remove the painted copper masks from their ravaged features to clean the red and puckered flesh beneath. Faces made as hollow as their souls by the horrors of war.

Some were luckier than others. One young man, who insisted to Adelaide that she call him Charlie, was missing his left eye, eyelid and all, and cheekbone. He wore a pair of glasses with plain lenses; affixed beneath the glass of the left side was a cunning fake eye contained within a thin copper plate painted to match his skin, complete with eyelashes. From across the room the effect was seamless. But as you moved closer, you saw that the glassy gaze could not follow you, and the edge where hard metal met soft flesh.

There was also the comical side effect that whenever he blinked it gave the impression of winking. Charlie himself remarked that he appeared to be flirting with anyone who looked in his direction.

There was a secrecy that surrounded McGowen and the Doctor; he had turned the cellar into what McGowen called a treatment room. A room they forbade Adelaide to set foot in.

Three out of the four patients residing at Ashthorne spent four hours every day in the bowels of the house. Once when she had dared asked McGowen what went on down there, Adelaide had been told that the Doctor was pioneering new treatments, and that her place was to care for the men when they were in their small ward.

The men, always quiet, speaking to Adelaide only to request help, were silent after the cellar sessions; after being bathed and fed, they would succumb to sleep.

Except Charlie, who never took part in those sessions and considered talking to be a competitive sport. In fact, she couldn't understand why he was still in need of convalesce. External wounds had healed. He was adjusted to his eye mask and the wooden leg; he made regular jaunts up and down the halls and was ready to try it on more challenging terrain outside.

During those four hours of the day in which they were left alone, Adelaide and Charlie's friendship flourished and, in a place as desolate as Ashthorne, they felt lucky to have found each other.

⟨CHAPTER TWO⟩

Adelaide awoke to an awful screaming, the likes of which she had never heard before. She had grown used to the wounded men's pained cries of anguish. This sound, however, she had only one point of comparison. She had been invited to a boxing day hunt once; it had only been the once, as she had made her distaste quite obvious after hearing the cries of a vixen separated from her pups. Adelaide remembered vividly the strangled cries as the hounds tore her asunder. The huntsmen had left the wretched thing in misery for fifteen horrible minutes before showing mercy with a bullet. A bullet might have been kinder to some of the men downstairs. At least they wouldn't have to relive the horrors every night.

Her mind snapped back to the present. McGowen was in charge of the men during the night-time hours: surely she must be attending to whoever it was right now.

14

What if it was Charlie? The screams weren't abating; they were escalating. Adelaide thought about the bottle of Veronal powder that was kept locked in the desk drawer on the ward. She suspected McGowen took a pinch in her afternoon cup of tea.

The lure of barbiturates could overcome the sensibility and reason of many a person, Adelaide knew this all too well. Her mother spent most of her days in a dazed stupor. The screams continued. Adelaide got out of the bed with enough force to cause the metal frame to scrape loudly across the floor. She looked at the gorges in the wood and cursed. McGowen made regular inspections of the room. She had no idea why, what difference did it make to her? It was all just another way to exert her power.

Adelaide wondered if she could move the bed to hide the scratches. She could worry about that later, though.

She walked across the room, mindful to tread carefully to minimise any noise. Futile, she knew; after the racket she'd made with the bed, being quiet now would not make a blind bit of difference. She reached the attic door and turned the handle. Nothing. The door held fast for a moment, before being flung inwards. McGowen stared back at her. Adelaide held her gaze for a moment, discombobulated, before finding her voice.

"I was just coming to help," she said. McGowen continued to stare.

"I heard the men screaming and," the words tumbled out, "I thought I could be of assistance."

"Everything is under control. Should I ever require your—assistance." McGowen heavily emphasised every syllable of the word, resulting in a fine spray on Adelaide's face. She resisted the urge to wipe the spittle from herself. "I shall inform you that I am in need of it. Understand?"

"Yes."

"I came up because of the god-awful noise you're making up here. Whatever it is you're doing, stop it immediately. You are disturbing our charges' rest."

Adelaide could barely suppress her laughter. The thought that she could disturb the people making those sounds simply by walking around was too much.

"I may have been too enthusiastic getting out of my bed. I was startled, but I shan't let myself react like that again." Adelaide said.

McGowen, regarding her once more with harsh disdain, only said, "See that you don't."

She whipped around with enough force to strike Adelaide's bare ankles with the heavy and stiff hem of her skirt, causing her to let out a small squeak of pain. McGowen, however, did not pay any heed and continued through the doorway. Once on the other side, the older woman turned back towards Adelaide, her hand gripping the handle as she said, "Goodnight, Miss Frost."

"Goodnight—" McGowen cut her off with the slam of the door.

ᚱ

Making her rounds the next morning, Adelaide paid close attention to the voices of each of the residents, trying to determine who she had heard screaming so awfully. It would be impossible to tell; the ones who did manage to communicate did so in such a subdued, faraway manner that it was as though their physical bodies were there, but something still trapped their voices in the trenches of France. As she tended to them, Adelaide thought of her own brother who had never come home, and felt a guilty twinge of gladness. Better buried in the ground than here amongst these forsaken creatures.

"I don't see why we have to house them. There must be dozens of suitable places in town."

The voice was that of a well-spoken young woman. Adelaide's ears pricked up, excited at the prospect of interacting with someone of her own sex and age.

"How could you ever have agreed to such a thing?"

"Evelyn, please contain yourself." This voice was older, male.

"No doubt it was that charlatan Roskopf that convinced you. If mother was still with us, he'd never would have sunk his talons into you. We should not leave these poor men under the care of one such as him."

Adelaide made her way into the hall where a stunningly beautiful woman stood arguing with an older, male version of herself. She could see that the elder Ashthorne had once been a very handsome man, but that a palpable sense of loss had ravished his beauty. Whilst that loss had caused the man's eyes to dull, his jowl to hang, it served to sharpen and highlight the woman. Eyes made hard by grief sparkled like sapphires. She held her jaw high and defiant as she challenged her father. The light from the hall's great door struck her fair hair, worn loose rather than in the customary chignon style expected of a woman her age, making it a tumbling cascade of red and gold. She was dressed simply, a twill vest and skirt in deep purple over a crisp white blouse. Whilst most woman would have a cameo broch or satin tie affixed to their collar, Evelyn's was undone. Combined with her loose hair, it lent her a rather rakish appearance.

A wolfspitz, all grey and white fluff, sat dutifully at her feet, letting out the occasional yap.

"I don't know how you dare bring your mother into this conversation! You went off gallivanting around the country the first chance you got. Where was your loyalty to her then? Personally, Evelyn, I don't think you're capable of it. I'm not discussing this any further."

Mr Ashthorne stalked away to his study, closing the door firmly behind him. Evelyn stood, her hand grasping the stair railing. Adelaide could see how the encounter with her father had affected her. Evelyn's breaths were coming in short rabid hitches and her eyes and cheeks shone wetly. She stood a moment longer before ascending the stairs and disappearing out of Adelaide's sight. The dog padded after her, his nails clattering on the marble floor.

CHAPTER THREE

There was a fresh addition on the ward.

Lucy, a youthful woman sent so there would always be someone on the ward day and night, and a gilt-framed mirror upon the wall.

Lucy, short, flaxen-haired, softly spoken, eye colour not yet determined as she continually stared at the floor. McGowen kept taking Lucy aside, murmuring to her. Adelaide couldn't hear their words, but by the smile on McGowen's face could surmise that she found Lucy far more agreeable than Adelaide. Anybody would be hard pressed to find Lucy offensive, even someone as odious as McGowen.

"I'll leave you in Miss Frost's hands. She'll introduce you to everyone."

McGowen scuttled out.

"I wouldn't worry too much about her, or the Doctor for that matter. They mainly leave me alone here," Adelaide said.

"What do they do then?"

"Honestly, I don't know. There's not that much to do here. Mostly it's being a friendly face, someone to talk to, not that any of them really talk that much. Wait 'til you met Charlie though, he can talk for all of us. Let's go."

Lucy stood, her eyes still cast towards the floor.

"I was nervous too, being away from home the first time, strange place, strange people. We'll look after one another and I'm sure we'll be the best of friends." The last part was a lie. Adelaide couldn't imagine wanting to spend any more time with this girl than was necessary.

Adelaide held out her hand and offered a smile. Lucy took it, Adelaide gave it a brief squeeze before dropping it. "I'm not going to walk in there, hand in hand with you. You still need to be able to muster a little respect from the man, but every time you feel a little nervous, just imagine that little squeeze I gave you. I guarantee it'll make you feel better."

They walked into the ward, Adelaide a step behind. She felt like a dog herding a lone lamb.

"Good morning, gentlemen," Adelaide said. As expected, there was no response to her cheery tone bar Charlie.

"Who have you got here with you Addy?"

"Charlie, this is Lucy—"

"Miss Cotton," Lucy said sharply in a pitch perfect imitation of McGowen's razor edged tone. Her meek walk transfigured into a cocky stride as she made her way to Charlie's bed.

She's not listened to a word.

Lucy had decided to emulate McGowen, but this new found self-assurance was soon halted as she reached the bed. Charlie had yet to put his mask on. The red puckered flesh, the empty socket and missing cheekbone, all on display.

Revulsion didn't briefly pass on Lucy's face, it took up residence. Charlie saw it too. Although he did his best not to reveal his upset, Adelaide saw the way he clutched at the blanket with his left hand, his knuckles as stark white as the bedsheet.

How would Lucy cope with urine stained sheets? With the blood, pus and other bodily fluids? Adelaide herself wasn't so naïve as not to recognise the evidence left by the men having "relieved" their tension by their own hand. The last thing they needed was to be shamed for doing so.

Adelaide didn't know if she trusted herself to speak. If she had the power, she'd be dragging Lucy out by the scruff of her neck.

"This is why you should knock. Give a bloke a chance to get himself looking decent."

"You, decent? An impossible task if ever there was one." Adelaide passed him the mask from the small nightstand beside his bed. She kept her gaze on Lucy, who watched in fascination as Charlie affixed it.

"I think I scrub up nicely."

"You're not bad, I suppose," Adelaide replied.

Charlie turned to Lucy.

"Well, I'm glad you're here, if only so I don't have to see —"

Adelaide held her hand up to her neck and shook her head. Charlie catching on straight away quickly changed course.

"Miss Frost every day."

"Yes, I'm sure Miss Frost will be grateful for the rest, Mr...?"

"Charlie is fine."

Lucy looked at Adelaide for an answer.

"I don't recall," she said, suppressing a smirk. "He's always been Charlie to me."

"I'll look it up. Surely the others shouldn't be allowed to sleep the day away?"

"They're not sleeping," Adelaide said. "They're just very quiet."

"So quiet," Charlie affirmed.

"Well," Lucy began, her imitation of McGowen was wavering though a quivering note underpinning the harshness. "There are obviously major failings going on here."

"I couldn't agree more, but I don't have the privilege or authority to do anything more than to make them as comfortable as possible and ensure that kindness and compassion is something that they get from me daily."

"That is the failing. Mrs McGowen believes you are making them soft with your fawning. How can anybody progress if they are not encouraged to fight?"

Adelaide was prepared there and then to show Lucy what it meant to fight, but just as she stepped towards her, ready to unleash a torrent of verbal lashings, McGowen stepped onto the ward.

"Miss Frost, now that Miss Cotton is here, why don't you take today off? It'll be so well deserved after all. I'll oversee things here."

There was a glint in her eyes as she spoke, and Adelaide knew the bitch had designed this situation both to piss her off and see how Lucy would carry out her instruction.

"Thank you," she muttered as she walked past McGowen, not trusting herself to say anything else.

ᚨ

Adelaide hadn't seen Evelyn again for a week after witnessing her argument with her father. She had gone to attend to a few affairs in Manchester.

Early on Sunday mornings, Adelaide had fallen into the habit of taking a pot of tea into the sunroom at the rear of the house, enjoying the solitude as she watched the sun creep its way across the lawn, bringing it from black to a deep emerald before settling on spring green. After which, she walked into the village.

On this morning, it startled her to find Evelyn sitting with her knees hugged to her chest, staring into the blackness. She was wearing Turkish trouser-style pyjamas in so dark a blue that they appeared almost black in the low light, yet Adelaide could see how frayed the cuffs were. Another sign of the Ashthornes' decline? The dog, Riley, sat beside her; at seeing Adelaide he leapt off the chair, his tail wagging as he walked up to her. He let out a friendly yap.

Evelyn turned towards Adelaide. In the minimal light, Adelaide could see the red rims encircling her eyes.

"What makes you think you have permission to be in here?" Evelyn was on her feet. Her voice wavered before taking on a more authoritative tone.

"You forget your place—"

"Adelaide Frost."

"Yes, Miss Frost. Just because you are in the employ of Roskopf does not give you permission to roam around. If you have no work to do here, then leave."

"I'm sorry to have disturbed you," Adelaide said, turning her back to Evelyn. "Oh, there's tea in the pot if you want it."

CHAPTER FOUR

The church was in complete disarray; stained glass from the smashed windows carpeted the floor, catching the light so they sparkled like crushed jewels. Someone had crudely hacked enormous chunks out of the back of the pews. Adelaide had passed by the church on her way to Ashthorne, and although she had not stopped to go inside, the previous time it'd had an air of warmth and welcoming. Now it felt cold and foreboding, something that went beyond a simple vandalism. A young woman was sweeping the shards into a pile, her lips pursed, tawny hair falling over furrowed brow.

"Can I help?" Adelaide picked up a dustpan and brush and started to clear the glass. It was a strangely pleasant change to have this to focus on. Adelaide found going into the village, which had been all but stripped of its male population, akin to drowning. You could feel the remnants of panic having long given way to an oppressive atmosphere of melancholy acceptance.

All the world had lost so many of their men and boys, had been left with the scars, but this place was a ragged and open wound.

The girl's eyes flicked up to meet Adelaide's, flashed in recognition, then fell to the floor again; she let out a humph sound and continued sweeping.

"What happened?"

"You ask a lot of questions," The girl said, not looking up from her work.

"I'd have thought more people would help, a community effort," Adelaide said brightly, determined to push through the girl's hostility.

"What do you know about community? Living in that gigantic house." Her tone held all the sharpness of the broken glass in it.

"It's a job," Adelaide said mildly.

The girl continued to sweep. "I'm Justine."

"Adelaide. I've seen you and your mother at the house."

"Do you enjoy living in Ashthorne?" The question surprised her. It certainly was a welcome distraction from her previous life back home, which lay in tatters. Not wanting to go too much into personal details, Adelaide settled on a vague answer.

"It's strange, being so far from home, but it's not too bad."

"Have you met Miss Ashthorne yet?"

Adelaide was growing accustomed to Justine's style of abruptly changing subjects.

"I've had the pleasure," Adelaide began, sensing an opportunity for bonding she added. "Spoilt and rude."

"She's not so bad. But watch out for her getting too friendly."

"How so?"

"Just be careful. I'm glad I don't have to be there more than a few hours a week." Justine glanced about the church, before lowering her voice. "Can you keep a secret?"

"Yes," Adelaide said.

"As soon as I've saved enough, I'm leaving this village. You should do the same. This place is rotten all the way through." Justine once again cast her eyes on the floor and the two women worked in silence.

ᚠᚦ

29

Adelaide was in the kitchen, mulling over her strange encounter with Justine whilst preparing a meagre supper,
when Evelyn, accompanied as always by Riley, approached
her.

"How long have you worked for them?"

"Pardon?"

"How long have you worked," Evelyn let out a sigh,
"for Roskopf and McGowen?"

"Do you speak to Lucy like this or am I special?" Adelaide could have sworn that Evelyn's lips almost curled into
a smile. "I've been working for Doctor—"

Evelyn held a hand up to stop her. "That man's not a
doctor."

"All I know is what I've been told. They gave him charge
of those patients—"

"Well, that's an arguable point." Evelyn said, not looking at Adelaide, but at some point behind her. Adelaide
turned to see McGowen fast approaching. The dog gave a
low growl.

"Miss Ashthorne, I trust your trip to the city was satisfactory. I didn't expect to find you back quite so soon,
though." She glared at the still growling dog who, to his
credit, continued to stand defiantly at Evelyn's side.

"Well, I know it inconveniences you and Mr Roskopf to have me and father in the house."

McGowen instantly prickled at Evelyn's insistent use of 'Mr'.

"The Doctor and I remain most gracious towards your father regarding the use of the house and grounds," McGowen said, her voice steeped in a sickly sweetness in stark contrast to her eyes, which, Adelaide thought, were incapable of hiding her contempt for everyone and everything that didn't revolve around her precious Doctor.

Adelaide decided she wasn't all too bothered about eating after all, and thus attempted to leave.

"No, stay," Evelyn said, as Adelaide tried to slip away. "I believe Elizabeth is just about to retire for the night." Evelyn held the woman's gaze. She was still the mistress of this house, and as much as it pained McGowen, she had no choice but to acquiesce.

"I suggest you are not late to your bed," McGowen said, addressing Adelaide. "I want the whole of the infirmary scrubbing down tomorrow."

She shot Evelyn one more look of barely disguised contempt, before marching off.

After making sure McGowen was out of earshot, Adelaide turned to Evelyn.

"I know this is your home, but I don't appreciate being told to sit and heel like I'm another of your lapdogs. I don't like the pair of them much either, but you've no right to be using me in your battles."

Evelyn studied Adelaide, who felt prickles of heat on her neck. She had quickly changed out of her uniform before coming down to eat. There seemed to be a hint of amusement in her eyes as she took in Adelaide standing there in threadbare grey trousers (her brother's) and a pale blue blouse (her own).

"It's been a long day," Adelaide said, not breaking eye contact. "I like to feel comfortable."

A slight, almost imperceptible nod of the head from Evelyn.

"Would you like to have dinner with me? More and more, father either dines alone in his study, or with Roskopf. I'd be glad for a little company. Also, I feel as if I owe you an apology. After all, Riley has taken to you, and I trust his judgement more than most." Evelyn smiled, the first time she had done so in front of Adelaide.

Beautiful. She is unearthly beautiful, Adelaide thought; so mesmerised was she that it took her a moment to realise that Evelyn had spoken again.

"I unfairly judged you and assumed that you were firmly in line with the two of them."

"What exactly have they done to offend you so?"

"Have dinner with me," Evelyn said, her eyes firmly on Adelaide's waiting for an answer. Sensing Evelyn's need for confirmation emboldened Adelaide.

"May I ask Miss Ashthorne who shall prepare this meal?"

"There's a roasted joint of beef in the refrigerator, and bread, it may not be much ... " Evelyn trailed off, awaiting Adelaide's reply.

"I'd be delighted to have a sandwich with you?" Adelaide silently cursed herself. What a stupid thing to say.

"Privacy would be nice. I don't trust Elizabeth to not walk in at any moment."

"We could go up to my room," Adelaide said hesitantly. "We'd be able to hear if anyone tried to climb the stairs, and Riley is more than welcome to come too."

"Go and freshen up whilst I prepare the food. I won't be long." Evelyn smiled again, and Adelaide thought that her heart would stop beating if she knew she would never see that smile again.

"It's not much, is it?"

"I thought it was lovely."

"I didn't mean the food," Evelyn said wistfully. "Although it stands true for that as well. I wish you could have seen the house as it was before mum died."

"The house is still magnificent, Miss Ashthorne, servants or not," Adelaide said, feeding the last of her sandwich to Riley.

"It's not just that. Mum was always so vibrant and full of life. She lit up the entire house. After she fell ill, well, I think that sickness spread to the very core of Ashthorne."

"How did your mother die?" Adelaide asked.

"It was influenza," Evelyn said, voice even and measured. "Father had heard of the illness in Manchester, so when mother took ill with it, he brought in Roskopf right away. He could not save her, though I suppose as a community we were lucky. When you think of the loss of life in other places. We only had the one. I wish I'd been here. I was away, down south on the coast. It took days for the message to reach me. I'd been flitting from place to place, and nobody was sure exactly where I was. I should've come home, but Father said she would get better, and there was no point in my getting ill as well."

Evelyn paused, staring blankly ahead. Adelaide couldn't think of anything appropriate to say. It struck her as odd that Evelyn's father would have had time to fetch a doctor and send word to Evelyn. In her experience, the influenza struck people down within days, sometimes hours.

Adelaide could see the pricks of tears form. When Evelyn looked up, her eyes looked like they'd been coated with diamond dust.

"I think father insisting on my not coming home was purely down to that man. Ever since then, Roskopf and his lackey Elizabeth have had the run of the house, and I can't understand why. I don't believe he helps any of those men. They claim that every day in that cellar, that they are curing those men of their illness. Adelaide, tell me honestly. Do you know what they do down there?"

Adelaide felt her cheeks burn. "I don't know."

"What are you doing here?"

"Sometimes I really don't know. I wanted to make a difference, but I just feel superfluous."

"Why do they not include you?"

"McGowen doesn't trust me, that I do know. Lucy—" Adelaide sighed, "Lucy's the most passive person I've ever met in my life. She's a perfect fit for them."

"I shouldn't spend too much time up here. Would you like to go for a walk in the grounds tomorrow?"

"I'd like that, but I'll be working."

"After you've finished then?"

Adelaide nodded in agreement.

Evelyn stood in one graceful movement, brushing the breadcrumbs off her skirt. Riley leapt down, sniffing each individual morsel out before devouring it.

"Until tomorrow, then."

"Yes, until tomorrow."

ᚠᚦ

Unbeknownst to Adelaide, Evelyn had conspired with Lucy to cover her duties.

"I want to show you this during the day," Evelyn said, when she collected Adelaide from the ward at midday. "And I couldn't wait till your day off, either."

As they left, Adelaide caught sight of Charlie. His real eye shone with amusement.

Evelyn led Adelaide to the kitchen and opened the door, exiting onto the rear of the house. Before they could walk out, Riley scrambled past them to relieve himself against the nearest oak. Feeling more comfortable, he bounded up the side of the house, a blur of white and grey fur, and out of view, happy to stretch his legs.

"Where are we going?" Adelaide called as Evelyn picked up her pace and cut across the lawn, towards the brook and over the small stone bridge.

"You'll see."

Trees lined the other side of the water, obscuring, despite their winter bare branches, the view of the other side.

Evelyn waited on the other side for Adelaide to catch up, before leading her down a brick path, weeds sprouting through the cracks, and through the trees.

"They act as a windbreak," Evelyn explained.

"For what?"

Adelaide had no sooner asked when she saw it. Iron and glass married together in a magnificent structure, which by Adelaide's estimation measured a hundred foot in length and forty in height. The conservatory sparkled in the low winter light.

"Wow, it's beautiful," Adelaide said, trying to reclaim her breath stolen by the whipping wind.

Riley raced past them and sat waiting at the door.

"Let's get inside," Evelyn took Adelaide gently by the hand. "You'll warm up once you're out of the wind."

The interior was packed full of plants of various species, all dead.

"I've been clearing it out bit by bit," Evelyn said, as she lit a camp stove and put water onto boil, "but I doubt we'll ever have enough funds to buy any more of the exotic plants, let alone heat the conservatory so they can thrive."

Riley settled on a blanket beside the stove, contented to be in a familiar place.

"What do you mean, heat it? Isn't that what the sun is for?"

"English sunshine can only stretch so far." Evelyn removed a small teapot and some mugs from the battered cabinet next to the stove. "No, to get the temperatures you need for the tropical plants, you need an external source of heat. There are miles of pipe snaking their way around us." She gestured round, her voice and eyes filling with passion. "They carried steam fuelled by a boiler built beneath."

Evelyn stepped closer to Adelaide. "Are you feeling any warmer?" she said, taking Adelaide's hands, her thumbs gently rubbing across her palms.

Adelaide gulped. She was feeling very warm indeed.

"I used to come in here all the time just to feel the heat. Even during the bitterest of winters, you'd come in here and feel the sweat drip down your back, so hot that you'd want nothing more than to strip off your clothing just so you could breathe."

Adelaide's chest tightened.

What would happen, she thought, *if I were to lean forward and kiss her?*

They stood locked in the moment. Evelyn had a glint in her eyes, as if daring Adelaide to act.

It would be so easy to entwine her fingers in Evelyn's hair, to tilt her head back, to feel the warmth of her lips upon her own.

To …

The moment shattered when the kettle whistled. Evelyn dropped Adelaide's hands and stepped away.

"Would you like some tea, Miss Frost? I believe there's some in the pot."

ᚠ

Evelyn made the tea, and they sat down to drink.

"I wouldn't have pegged you as a gardener," Adelaide said, taking a sip of her drink. All the previous formalities now shed.

39

"Well, as I said, this used to be the warmest place you could be, and you know how bloody cold that house gets, especially when you're alone in bed at night."

Adelaide spluttered on her drink, earning a look of wry amusement from Evelyn. Had she said that on purpose? There was certainly that damn beautiful smile on her face. A smile that Adelaide just knew would be her undoing.

"There's a satisfaction in watching something grow from nothing. The gardeners gave me my plot to look after when I wasn't at school. Mum would encourage me to tend to it, to love it. I think it was her way of teaching me patience. I don't think any of that rubbed off on any other aspect of my life, but I can plant a seed and be content with knowing it will be awhile before anything comes of it."

Evelyn moved closer, glancing around before lowering her voice to a conspiratorial whisper.

"Adelaide, would you be willing to help me?"

I'd be willing to do anything for you, Adelaide thought. She nodded once in confirmation.

"I need to know what they are doing down there. This man calls himself a medical man, but what proof has he offered? Do you hear the screaming at night?" Again, Adelaide nodded. "Those men are not getting better, they are getting worse. If I were to distract them, you could go down into the cellar, see what kind of equipment he has down there."

"When?" Adelaide asked.

"Tomorrow, Lucy will be on the ward. I'll convince father we should all dine together. That'll give you ample time to get down and have a look around." Evelyn clasped Adelaide's hand. "Thank you so much for doing this. We ought to get back to the house now. I'll come to your room tomorrow night, and you can tell me what you saw."

41

CHAPTER FIVE

Adelaide was splitting her concentration between keeping her face in a neutral expression and cleaning out the empty eye socket. Smiling could condescend, sorrow seemed insincere; during the most intimate moments Adelaide found it was best to maintain detachment. Sergeant Dominic Dugdale regarded Adelaide with one mud-coloured eye. His injury extended across his cheek, upper lip, and nose; there was so little of his original features left. Finished, Adelaide replaced the mask. Only then did she smile.

"Thank you." His voice was low, ghostly.

Adelaide reached for his hand and gave it a gentle squeeze. She desperately wanted to ask what happened in the treatment room but said, "Can I get you anything else?"

Dominic shook his head softly and turned away from her. She stood up, cleaning the basin of water and pus-streaked cotton wads away.

"Miss Frost?" the voice belonged to Charlie, as always soft-spoken and heartbreakingly polite. He held a deck of cards aloft. Adelaide quickly finished tidying, then settled on the edge of the bed. Charlie scooted back into a cross-legged position and dealt. Adelaide loved these moments. They reminded her of rainy afternoons spent with her brother before the war.

Charlie reminded Adelaide of her brother in a myriad of ways: masculine with a sensitive edge. He was a man who, in different circumstances, would have found himself a clerk's job with a bank, a man who would have found an adoring wife. A man whose children would idolise him as a benchmark of decency.

"How's she treating you?" Charlie always referred to McGowen as anything other than by her name. He was being especially genial today with his choice of 'she'. Adelaide had heard him say much worse things.

"Same as always," Adelaide replied, gathering her cards. "Like I'm something nasty she's trodden in."

"Well, I'm glad you're here, and not just because you're god awful at cards and I love winning." Adelaide knew what Charlie meant. There was something irreparably broken in the other men which had incredulously survived in Charlie

43

despite the destruction of his body. Playing cards and chatting helped him cling onto normality.

"Where did you go with that woman yesterday? Boy, is she a looker! I'm going to have to brush off the old olive drab." Charlie pulled at the collar of his pyjamas. "All the ladies love a man in uniform."

"If I weren't that little bit older than you ..."

"Addy, no, that would be too close to incest," he said, mouth dropping in faux horror. "Anyhow I much prefer that maid."

"Mrs Lennox?" she teased.

"No, the young one. She's so feisty."

Like Evelyn. A tinge of excitement ran through Adelaide at the thought of her. She couldn't wait to see her, even though she didn't know what Evelyn expected to find down there, in the cellar, but she was glad to have an excuse to spend time with her. Charlie and Adelaide fell into silence as they continued their game, but she couldn't shake the feeling of dark eyes on the back of her head.

ᚠᚦ

Justine, Charlie's potential paramour, was a damn sweetheart compared to her mother, whose level of acridness was nothing like Adelaide had ever encountered before. Just a look from her was enough to fill your mouth with a bitter taste.

Whilst Justine scurried around the house, cleaning, Mrs Lennox seemed to be perpetually peeling vegetables.

"You!" she raised her knife and pointed towards Adelaide. "That lad who Justine's taken a shine to?"

"What about him?" Adelaide asked.

Mrs Lennox stayed silent.

"What about him?" she reasserted.

"Apart from being an outsider ..."

She trailed off. *Because she's remembered that I'm an outsider as well.*

"He's a good man," she said. "Charlie will always be kind to Justine and—"

"Justine had a brother."

Everybody had a brother, a son, a father.

"I'm sorry for your loss."

"He would have had a happy life. I won't let Justine's be ruined."

Adelaide bit down on the urge to protest. If anything, Charlie was too good for Justine.

"Edward has really brought this village back together. We lost so many, but he'll make sure that'll never happen again."

"Who's Edward?"

No answer. Mrs Lennox put her head down and started to dice an onion. Justine had certainly inherited her mother's abrupt manner of ending a conversation.

ᚠᚦ

Adelaide spent the rest of the day in a state of restlessness, going through her few duties mechanically. At six o'clock, Lucy came to relieve her. The cellar of Ashthorne House was most unusual in having two separate staircases: one in the kitchen, and a second just down the hall from the men's infirmary. She thought it best to go down to the kitchen entrance, lest Lucy mention her trespassing to McGowen or Roskopf. She wouldn't put it past her to go running to them straight away, interrupting their dinner with Evelyn and her father.

Adelaide crept down the stairs, fearful that one or the other, or both, would appear behind her, demanding to know what it was she thought she was doing. She reached the bottom of the stairs, the lantern in her hand shaking, casting all manner of shadow beasts on the wall. It didn't take long for Adelaide to realise that her efforts were for naught. The part of the cellar connected to the kitchen was an entirely separate entity to that which Roskopf had access to.

It was obvious that the two rooms had once been one; an archway had been bricked in, the mortar was pale, the red brick vibrant. By Adelaide's reckoning, it had been done sometime within the last six months. There was no way she could access the other half, not without being seen.

This, when she told Evelyn, would only strengthen her belief that something was being hidden. And God only knew what Evelyn would ask of her next.

ᚠᚦ

Adelaide thought her failure to find out any new information would disappoint Evelyn, yet she had never seen Evelyn look so elated. In fact, she was feeling queasy, watching as Evelyn paced back and forth, all the while wildly gesticulating.

"I was right. I knew it all along." Evelyn stopped in front of Adelaide and gripped her by the shoulders. "Do you realise what this means?" Adelaide shook her head. "It means that when I prove to father that Roskopf is an absolute charlatan he can be out of this house."

Along with me, Adelaide thought.

"You still need proof that he's actually doing something wrong. Just because you don't agree with his methods ..."

"Trust me when I say I know. Why go to such lengths to hide what they're doing if it's so innocent? Bricking up passages without permission." Evelyn's mood darkened briefly, before brightening again. "Let's go down tonight."

"Excuse me?"

"If we go down around one or two in the morning, everyone will be dead to the world. We could sneak down. Prove that it's nothing more than a torture chamber. When I tell father, he'll demand to see, and Roskopf will have no choice but to leave."

"This is madness." Adelaide said.

"It will be exciting," Evelyn countered.

Adelaide understood then that they had more in common than she initially thought. To Evelyn, this was a source of adventure, of escaping just as Adelaide herself had done by joining the Red Cross. She tried to imagine what it must have been like in this house, so far from any kind of social interaction. Evelyn had spoken briefly of friends made during her time at boarding school, but her education had ended

48

years ago. Adelaide wondered why Evelyn stayed at Ashthorne. Was it an obligation to her dead mother to look after her father? Evelyn had the charm, beauty, and intelligence to live an independent life. Although that would mean she'd have to work. Adelaide decided she'd just have to indulge Evelyn once more.

"What exactly do you propose we do?"

Evelyn beamed. "Well, first of all it needs to be a night you're working. Then, you come to my room after midnight."

CHAPTER SIX

At twenty minutes past midnight, Adelaide crept out of the ward and towards Evelyn's room, knocking gently on the door until she heard a hushed, "Come in."

Evelyn was in her nightclothes in the dim light. Adelaide took in the exposed pale skin of the curve of her neck, ivory silk clinging to the curve of her breasts; the way her pale hair cascading down her back took on a silvery glint in the moonlight streaming through the window.

"Sorry, should I leave whilst you get dressed?" she stammered.

Riley jumped off the bed and trotted over to her, pressing his muzzle into her hand.

"No, it's fine I'm going like this." Adelaide's gaze fell to Evelyn's breasts, aware of herself staring, she snapped her head back to look Evelyn in the face.

Evelyn was staring right back at her.

She felt the heat rise from the back of her neck to her brow. Ashamed of having been caught so openly ogling, Adelaide started to apologise. Evelyn stopped her by raising one finger to her mouth and pressing it gently to her lips.

"There's no time for embarrassment. Did you hear anything on your way up?"

"No, I'm quite certain that everyone's sleeping." Adelaide said, still feeling the blood boiling in her cheeks.

"Good, let's go then."

ᚠᚦ

Adelaide had never known how fast her heart could beat before now, as she and Evelyn made their way down the stairs. The cellar door was just down the hall from the ward. Conveniently placed, so she had never seen the men coming and going.

Adelaide's chest almost burst when she saw the lock empty of the key, only to be assured when Evelyn produced it out of nowhere. Evelyn turned the key, the click deafeningly loud in the hall's silence. They made their way down the steps gingerly. Safe, knowing they couldn't be seen, Evelyn lit the lamp she had been carrying to reveal nothing. Her face dropped, first in confusion, then disappointment.

"What exactly were you expecting?" Adelaide said hesitantly. Evelyn didn't answer. In the dim glow of the lamp, Adelaide could see the pinpricks of tears forming in Evelyn's eyes. She wiped them away.

"I feel very foolish. What did I think I'd find down here? A cat-o'-nine-tails and a rack?"

"Evelyn, maybe Roskopf isn't a competent doctor, but that doesn't mean he is actively evil. I think you give him more credit than he deserves. He's quite the bumbling idiot, really. McGowen, on the other hand …" Evelyn smiled. "Also, is it me or does this room look smaller than it ought to be?"

Just then, footsteps started emanating from above, followed by the sound of McGowen's voice: "I am resolute that I heard one of them scurrying about."

"If they were, they've calmed down now," a deeper voice answered.

"Where is that girl? She's been getting friendly with Evelyn—"

Upon hearing the movement above, Evelyn had quickly shut her oil lamp off. In the darkness, she fumbled for Adelaide's hand. Finding it, she pulled Adelaide close. The sounds above faded away.

Deprived of sight, Adelaide became hyper aware of Evelyn's balmy hands, her racing heartbeat pounding against her chest. She felt her own heartbeat rise in response as she slipped an arm around Evelyn's waist, drawing her closer in. Close enough now to smell the cinnamon and clove tooth powder Evelyn used. Evelyn let out a whimper.

"It'll be ok," whispered Adelaide, "don't be afraid."

"I'm not." Evelyn's voice was heavy, husky in her ear. Emboldened by the dark, Adelaide turned her head, searching for Evelyn's lips. She found them. Almost instantly, the pleasure receded, and fear took hold of her.

Had she misread Evelyn? Adelaide stilled, waiting for Evelyn to show her what she wanted. She expected Evelyn to push her away, to rebuke her for her brashness. Instead, she felt a steady hand slide up her back to her neck as strong fingers entwined themselves in her hair, drawing her back into the kiss.

Eventually, but still too soon for Adelaide, Evelyn broke away. "I think they've gone." Adelaide listened carefully. Evelyn was right, Roskopf and McGowen, apparently satisfied nothing was amiss had departed for their beds.

"Maybe we should leave too. I don't know about you, but my feet are freezing." Evelyn turned the lamp back on.

Without another word, she caught Adelaide's hand and led them both back up the cellar stairs.

ᚠᚦ

The day after their kiss in the cellar of Ashthorne house, Evelyn's father requested she accompany him to Manchester whilst he attended to business there.

Adelaide had seen them both as they were leaving; Evelyn had smiled politely towards Adelaide before her face settled into a mask of neutrality. Evelyn had seemed more than welcoming of Adelaide's advance, yet she worried now that Evelyn had chosen to gloss over the incident, perhaps chalking the kiss up to a lapse of judgement caused by a mix of excitement and fright. She decided she wouldn't broach the subject again; she'd leave it up to Evelyn.

The house, always quiet, felt barren and stark to her now with Evelyn absent.

Adelaide sensed another subtle shift that had occurred. Since she and Evelyn had gone down to the cellar that night, Adelaide felt McGowen's eyes upon her continually, and the previously taciturn McGowen now attempted to engage her in conversation constantly. No doubt trying to catch her out.

That McGowen was now paying attention to her made Adelaide feel very uneasy.

When asked where she had been that night, she maintained she had needed to answer the call of nature.

It certainly lent weight to Evelyn's theory of nefarious doings on McGowen's and Roskopf's part. She wished Evelyn would come home.

CHAPTER SEVEN

Adelaide was bitterly cold. Her breath hung above her as she curled round onto her side, wrapping her thin blanket around her tightly: the last thing she wanted was to get out of bed. She looked towards the window; even in the near dark, she could see the frost that covered it inside and out.

She thought of Evelyn saying how cold a bed is when you're alone in it, and how warm Evelyn would feel curled up next to her. Knowing that she could no longer delay the inevitable, she got up and dressed.

ᚠᚦ

Justine was on the ward polishing the mirror. Because of its massive size, she stood precariously on a chair. Even with the extra height, she was on her tiptoes, reaching into the corners with her cloth. Adelaide felt nervous just watching her.

"They haven't made it easy for you, have they?" she said, holding a hand out to help Justine down.

"It's a monstrosity," Justine said, taking her hand.

"I like it," Adelaide said, for no other reason than to interject something positive into the exchange.

"It matches nothing else."

"True, and why put it in here, of all places? But it's a beautiful piece."

"Well, I'm glad I don't have to touch it again." Justine wrapped her arms around herself, and, as though the mere thought of the mirror conjured chills, shivered.

"It feels strange, touching it. It's hard to explain—it's a tightness of the chest and it's so—so cold."

"The entire house is freezing," Adelaide said, attempting to comfort her.

"Have you touched it?"

Adelaide hadn't. Despite its beauty, she was repelled by it, by the impossible shadows that danced across its surface.

"Well, no, I haven't—" She couldn't tell Justine that it frightened her. "I wouldn't want to leave smear marks all over it."

"I better be getting on with my work."

"Would you like to go to the teahouse?" Adelaide wanted to talk to Justine outside the house, to grasp on to a little bit of normality. Despite having fled her old life, there were certain aspects she missed.

"No, thank you."

"I'll pay."

"No, thank you."

"Let me know if you change your mind. It would be nice to have a friend, to get out of the house."

Justine stalked out of the room, leaving Adelaide to wonder what she had done wrong. She stared at herself in the mirror. Slowly she reached out; her fingertips hovered millimetres from the glass, so close to that reflected world, but she couldn't bring herself to touch it.

ᚠᚹ

The sunroom continued to be Adelaide's favourite place in the house—until, that was, McGowen decided that the sunroom was also her perfect spot. She was sitting reading when McGowen strolled into the room and positioned herself opposite her. She glanced up from her book, hoping that a small smile and nod would be sufficient. McGowen was not content.

"How are you finding it here?"

"I like it here." Adelaide closed her book, placing it on the seat beside her. "The work is satisfying; the house is beautiful. I'm even making friends."

"Evelyn?"

"I've spoken a few times with Evelyn. but I was talking more about Justine; she has some interesting views about the house and the village. I'd like to hear more of them." McGowen's face twisted slightly at this, as if she were afraid of what Justine could tell her.

"I'd like to know more about you, Adelaide. What do you do with your free time?"

"I like to do what I'm doing now, read. Enjoy the view from this room—"

"I meant," McGowen let out an exasperated sigh, "what do you get up to at night? Must be lonely up there by yourself?"

"Most nights I'm so tired I just fall right to sleep."

"No midnight excursions?" McGowen's mouth twitched. The sun hitting her eyes made them seem to glow with malevolence.

"No," Adelaide said firmly. She picked her book back up, signalling that the conversation was over.

59

CHAPTER EIGHT

Evelyn spent an entire month in Manchester, leaving Adelaide a nervous wreck for the entirety of it. The day when she heard Evelyn was due back, she'd taken every opportunity to rush to her attic bedroom, and from its small window had furtively scanned the peaks, searching for the Ashthornes' car.

Evelyn finally arrived home late in the afternoon.

Later that night, Adelaide crept down to Evelyn's room and gently knocked.

"Come in."

As soon as Adelaide was through the door, Evelyn enveloped her in her arms.

"I missed you," she murmured against Adelaide's neck

"I missed you too. I was so worried that you regretted—"

Before she could finish her sentence, Evelyn had caught her lips with her own. A wave of relief washed over Adelaide, followed by an ever-growing heat emanating from between her legs.

She'd had been so focused on the kiss that she hadn't noticed Evelyn's hand had hitched up her nightgown, her thumb tracing the curve of her pelvis towards her centre. She gasped as Evelyn's fingers brushed against her.

"Why don't you show me how much you've missed me," Evelyn said, her hand now achingly far away. She moved towards the bed, sitting on the edge as she patted the space beside her. "Are you waiting for a formal invitation?"

Adelaide quickly closed the distance between them, pushing Evelyn so that she lay on the bed, capturing both of Evelyn's wrists, pinning them above her head as she kissed her. Through the thin material of their nightdresses, she could feel Evelyn's nipples harden and her quickening heartbeat.

Adelaide broke away. "Are you happy with this?"

Evelyn smiled, "Do you think you'd still be on top of me, if I wasn't?" she pulled Adelaide back down into the kiss, her hands trailing over the curve of her hips and up her back, digging her nails in. Adelaide let out a low growl as she pressed her thigh between Evelyn's legs.

"God, I've wanted you," Adelaide whispered. "Since the first moment I saw you, I wanted you."

"Then have me."

ᚠᚦ

Adelaide pulled Evelyn close to her, one arm wrapped around her waist, the other stroking her thigh.

"I should go. If anyone sees me leave your room—"

"I think you forget, Miss Frost, that I am the mistress of this house. To hell with what anyone thinks."

"Not even your father?"

"He knows what I am. He wouldn't be as shocked as you'd imagine."

"So that night in the cellar when we kissed ... That wasn't your first time?"

"There were two at boarding school. And two or three in Manchester. A maid, back when we had them."

Adelaide's hand left its resting place on Evelyn's thigh to point in feigned shock at her.

"So, it's a habit of yours to seduce the help."

Evelyn batted playfully at Adelaide's hand. "You make it seem as if I grossly abuse my power. And anyway, you don't work for my family, so it doesn't count."

"Wait, you're not talking about Justine, are you?" She said the words half in jest, but what if a failed romance between the two of them was the cause of Justine's hostility?

"No, she's not my type and I am most definitely, emphatically in fact, not hers."

Satisfied she would not be competing with Justine, Adelaide grasped Evelyn's waist, pulling her closer.

"You said your father knows who you are, but you never said how he felt about it."

"He tolerates it. Mum said she could tell from my being a little girl. She didn't care; always said she loved me, made father see he'd have to accept me as I am."

"Tell me more, she sounds like she was a wonderful woman," Adelaide said, trailing her fingers idly across Evelyn's stomach.

"She was the least judgmental person I'm ever likely to meet in my life. Even after I got sent home from boarding school, two different schools that is, she did nothing less than support me."

"May I hazard a guess that your expulsions were to do with your relationships with those two girls you mentioned?"

"Only the first time, After that, mother warned me I'd have to learn to be more discreet. No, the second time was because I was distributing suffrage literature."

"I think I may be falling for you even more, Miss Ashthorne." Realisation dawned on her. "That night we went down into the cellar, you wore the gown instead of pyjamas on purpose. Didn't you?"

"I had my suspicions about you. I wanted to make sure. What about you? You can't tell me that was your first time."

"What makes you say that?" Adelaide lilted, brushing her fingertips across Evelyn's stomach.

"I'm not shy about paying compliments when due. That was far too pleasurable to be beginner's luck."

"There was a girl, once. Apart from you, nobody else has ever known."

"You've never spoken about your family."

"My mother was never as present as yours." She sighed, withdrawing her fingers from Evelyn's stomach. "She was always in the house, in body, but the spirit was elsewhere. After my brother died, she somehow got worse. She swallowed down anything she could get a hold of: booze, pills, anything that would take her away. Anything I got up to slipped right by her."

"What about your father?"

"Preoccupied with work, worked his way up from bank clerk to manager."

"So, you're part of the nouveau riche?" Evelyn teased.

"I knew you'd pull class on me."

"Ashthorne has only survived by selling off the land piece by piece. Two generations ago, we had a coal pit, and for a time it was profitable. The bed was small though, and it was all gone within ten years from first sinking. By all accounts, my father spent a considerable chunk of his inheritance building this house. The only source of income now is the textile mill in Manchester."

"That doesn't sound so bad."

"It shouldn't, but from what I can find out, the mill should provide more than enough for us, yet between the source and this household, that money is disappearing."

"And you suspect Roskopf is responsible," Adelaide said.

"It's the only reasonable explanation."

"Whilst you've been away, McGowen has spoken to me more than the entire time I've been here. I think they both know we went down into the cellar that night." Adelaide paused. "Have you ever thought of moving? Travelling, maybe?"

"Why do you say that?"

"Because this house reminds you of your loss, because it makes you unhappy?"

"Maybe one day I'll leave and never come back. For now, though," Evelyn snuggled into the nape of Adelaide's neck, "I've found an excellent reason to stay."

ᚠᛈ

Despite Evelyn's sleepy protests, Adelaide removed herself from the warm bed, and arms that enveloped her, to go back to her attic room.

"Stay, just a while longer." Adelaide could hear that wicked smile. "I'll make it worth your while."

"Unlike some," she bent down to kiss Evelyn's forehead, "I have to get ready for work, and I don't have any of my clothes here."

"Your argument is flawed; you don't need clothes."

"I'll see you this afternoon."

Adelaide slipped out the door, closing it gently behind her. Lucy would be the only one awake, sitting guard at the desk, not doing much else. Until last night, she had thought it unfair that they rarely swapped shifts, but now the prospect of not being able to spend evenings and nights with Evelyn made any sympathy for Lucy fade away.

Thanks to Ashthorne's many windows, although dark, it was not pitch as she made her way carefully along the hall.

A shadow fell against the wall, the slight sound of padding feet on the wooden floor.

"If you've come to take me back to bed ..." she whispered as she turned around.

Evelyn was not there.

The sound of footsteps, a soft shuffling gait as if they dragged something behind them.

Go back.

Adelaide pressed on; Evelyn may have been safe in her bed, but there were plenty others in the house that could be walking about.

What about the shadow?

That impossibly dark shadow that moved alongside her; that turned the already frigid air into icy crystals.

"You're tired," she said to the shadow that danced upon the walls in time to that soft shuffle, a shuffle that was picking up speed.

Adelaide turned back, back to the warmth and light of Evelyn. The shadow was there in front of her, flicking like a flame.

She ran, her thudding steps a counterpoint to their shoe dogging swim. The shadow fell away behind her as she neared Evelyn's door. She slowed to a walking pace. That was her first mistake.

She stopped for a moment, waiting for her heart rate and breathing to return to normal. She didn't want Evelyn to think her a fool scared of her own shadow. She took several deep breaths, looking at her feet. Composed, Adelaide reached for the handle. Gone, replaced by inky darkness. The entire door was enveloped in a wide, gaping maw. The shadow vibrated, its edges blurring, the dragging swish morphing into a hum.

You're dreaming, open the door and it will be fine.

Adelaide grasped the handle and screamed.

ᚠᚦ

Evelyn and Adelaide crouched by the dying embers of the fire, whilst Evelyn gingerly examined the red and puckered tips of her right hand. Riley had left his bed and snuggled into Adelaide's lap.

"I warned you how cold this house gets in the winter, but I never thought it could give you frostbite—"

"Frost nip," she said gently. "When it isn't serious it's only frost nip, I'll be alright."

"Good, because I'm the only one who should be allowed to nip you, Miss Frost." She brought Adelaide's hand to her lips, gently kissing the palm. "I still don't understand how this happened."

Adelaide didn't understand either, could only recall the burning shooting up her arm, when she took hold of the handle, the scream before blessed numbness.

"Metal gets cold."

Evelyn's brow furrowed in amusement. "Indeed, it does, but that quickly? You closed that door behind you not two minutes before."

"You told me to stay. I should have listened," Adelaide said.

"Yes, you should have," Evelyn murmured. She still looked troubled by the incident. How could Adelaide add to that worry with talk of phantom shadows?

She reached out with her free hand, pushing back the hair that fell over Evelyn's brow. "It's fine, I promise."

"Next time you spend the night, you can bring your clothes for the morning with you."

"So, there will be a next time?"

"Oh yes, there will be a next time."

⟨HAPTER NINE

Sergeant Dugdale skipped up and down the ward under the watchful eye of the Doctor. Hysterical gait, he called it, one of the many manifestations of war neuroses.

It was a rare occasion that Dr Roskopf graced his patients with his presence. Adelaide had read of these neuroses in her friend's letters; the common treatment of them was work therapy. Small, simple tasks designed to stimulate the mind.

Roskopf, however, seemed content to merely observe. Aside from his work with the prosthetics, Adelaide had learned that he'd set up a small workshop in his quest to perfect them, and while she agreed this was worthwhile work, it did little to help them now.

It was clear why Evelyn thought he was a charlatan.

ᚠᚢ

"Do you have any puzzles?"

Evelyn furrowed her brow in thought.

"Boxes, jigsaws?"

"I know what you meant," Evelyn laughed. "I was merely thinking where I'll find any, but I'm sure there must be some somewhere. Do I not keep your hands occupied enough, Miss Frost?"

"It's for Charlie and the others. I know that not enough is done here for them."

"We'll find something. If not, the village has a little shop that sells trinkets and gifts."

ᚠᚢ

Luckily, a trip to the village was avoided when Evelyn appeared the next morning with a box.

"I haven't checked it," she said, putting it down on the end of Charlie's bed.

Charlie immediately started rummaging through the box, pulling out a jigsaw puzzle.

"Can you guarantee that all the pieces are in here?"

"No."

He dropped it back in. "This looks interesting!"

71

In his hand, he held a knot of interlocking shapes of polished wood. "Must be a way of disconnecting them," he murmured as he continued to fiddle with the object.

"Thank you so much for finding these," Adelaide said. "I think they'll get a lot of enjoyment out of them."

"No problem," Evelyn said, before leaning in towards Adelaide and whispering. "I'll see you later for a little enjoyment of our own."

Adelaide felt the heat rising in her and knew by the look in Evelyn's eyes and the sly smile that she must be blushing.

"Miss Frost, Charlie."

"Bye," Charlie muttered distractedly.

"Well, at least you'll be kept out of mischief for a while." Adelaide said, her eyes lingering on Evelyn's behind as she walked away, a few seconds more than was safe.

"I've never seen anything like this." Charlie said.

"What!"

"This puzzle."

"Can I look?"

Charlie handed it to her. It was extraordinary. Spirals, circles, triangles, along with shapes that resembled elongated Ws all entwined together.

"Huh."

"What?"

"Just seems familiar," she said, passing it back to Charlie.

ᚠᚦ

Although Evelyn had declared she didn't care who knew about their affair, Adelaide still practised caution; after all, her being here was conditional. Any moral misconduct, and this would certainly be regarded as so by McGowen, would result in her dismissal. Adelaide couldn't deny that it added an extra layer of excitement though, making her way through the house unseen to find Evelyn waiting for her. Sometimes she was clad in her nightclothes for Adelaide to finish undressing her, luxuriously slow; other times already fully naked, clawing at Adelaide's clothes, desperate to get her in the same state.

Once, Evelyn had come up to the attic, managing somehow to make love on Adelaide's small bed without falling off. Evelyn had declared it the most uncomfortable yet still pleasurable experience of her life, albeit one that she would rather not repeat.

"You smile a lot more than you used to," Charlie observed during one of their card games, "and it's ever since

Evelyn came back, funnily enough. You spend a lot of time together, don't you?"

"How do you know that, don't tell me she's sneaking in here at night? I'm not a jealous woman, but I will—"

"I may only have one eye, but that doesn't mean I don't see things. The way you blush for example. Plus, Justine told me."

"Justine?"

"Yes, she's been coming to see me on your days off, and after you've gone in the evenings. Once you get past the gruffness, she's really very sweet."

"You've had more luck than me. I've tried to be friendly to no avail. Maybe you could find out if I've offended her?"

"She told me—Addy, she told me you make her feel uncomfortable." Charlie looked around; the other men were all still dozing. "She thought you were trying to get her into your bed. I told her you're not like that, that the bitch was telling lies about you because she doesn't like you."

"This came from McGowen. That I'm some kind of deviant."

"Adelaide, I know about you and Evelyn. I told Justine she was just being spiteful, because I knew she wouldn't understand or accept it. The things I've seen … there are much worse things in this world than the idea that two women can be together."

Charlie's eye took on a faraway look.

"Men got lonely in the trenches. I think when you can die at any moment, you'll cling on to whatever you can. Fuck the fact that if they caught you, they'd punish you. Every day was already a punishment."

"Charlie, I never wanted to make Justine uncomfortable. It was an attempt at friendship, nothing more."

"I know that. The bitch was dripping poison into her ear. Justine knows better now. Next time you talk it'll be better."

"Thank you."

"Adelaide, if it wasn't for you, I don't know if I ever would have had the bollocks to even talk to her. When I'm well, I'm going to take her dancing, I'm going to show her a life beyond this place."

Adelaide swelled with joy to hear Charlie talk of a future, not just for himself, but as part of a couple.

She glanced up from her cards. Why was Charlie's breath visible?

The chill invaded the air with insidious tendrils of ice which ensnared her heart, her lungs arched with each fresh intake. Charlie was shivering now. The thin pyjamas which the men wore were no protection against the frigid air.

"Quick, get under your blanket." Adelaide tried to grasp the material to pull over Charlie, fighting against fingers rendered dumb by cold.

In the scramble to get Charlie undercover, her hand brushed against the wooden puzzle and, even in her panic, she registered that it was exceptionally warm.

Once Charlie was safe undercover, Adelaide looked around to check on the other men. They had not awoken, though they violently shivered; she could see the plumes of breath bellowing from them.

"Adelaide, the mirror," Charlie said, through chattering teeth.

Ice crystals were forming rapidly across the mirror's surface. It reminded Adelaide of fireworks, the way they bust out from multiple points of origin until all of it was covered. The silence pressed heavily, oppressing all thought but one from Adelaide, that she would freeze to death in this room. Adelaide wanted nothing more than to sleep, to drift off into oblivion. Then, as suddenly as it began, the cold receded. The frost retreated rapidly from the mirror's surface, water droplets running down in rivulets and pooling on the floor.

"What the bloody hell was that?" Charlie said.

Adelaide couldn't answer. She was too busy staring at the man in the next bed's blue lips and pallid skin.

ᚠᛈ

Evelyn, Charlie, and Adelaide had spent the past half hour staring at the mirror. None of them could come up with an explanation as to why the room had plunged into such extreme cold that it had killed a man.

"Even January in the trenches never got as cold as that," Charlie had said when he and Adelaide were describing to Evelyn what had happened.

Riley had accompanied Evelyn onto the ward; he had barked and growled at the mirror for five minutes before Evelyn picked him up and, to both his and Charlie's delight, deposited him on Charlie's bed.

"He never stood a chance, weak as he was." Adelaide shivered involuntarily at the memory. She could still feel icy tendrils caressing at her spine. "The cold … it came from the mirror." She took a deep breath as she prepared to voice for the first time what she thought to be insanity.

"From the moment they hung that mirror, the atmosphere, the entire tone of the room changed. I feel watched, like something is burrowing into my head. From the corner of my eyes, I see dark shapes dancing." Adelaide noticed her hands were shaking; she hadn't dared look at Charlie and Evelyn whilst she spoke for fear of ridicule, but their faces were a mixture of compassion and interest.

"There's no other way to say it then," Charlie announced. "I think there's something evil about it."

Adelaide loved Charlie that little bit more in that moment

"I wonder what's on the other side of the wall?" Evelyn said, seemingly more to herself than Adelaide and Charlie.

"You mean you don't know?" Charlie asked.

"I was away at school a lot and when I was home, I always found other sources of entertainment." A sheepish grin crossed her face; Adelaide knew exactly what entertainments she was referring too.

"House I grew up in. I knew every square inch, not that it was much bigger than this room. How the other half live, eh Addy? Maybe I ought to have snagged myself a bit of posh."

Evelyn's brow furrowed in confusion.

"He guessed." Adelaide said.

Evelyn grasped Adelaide's hand. "Well, there's something to be said for a bit of rough."

Charlie snorted with laughter.

"It's not funny. My father is a bank clerk, I'll have you know!"

Adelaide's faux indignity at being called common caused Evelyn and Charlie to descend into peals of much needed laughter, which cleared away the last remnants of tension.

"We're getting away from the matter here. There's something strange about that mirror, and we need to find out what it is." At this, Evelyn strode from the room. Adelaide heard the rattle of a locked door being tried before Evelyn walked back in.

"Wouldn't your father have a key?" Adelaide said.

"There'll be one in his study. He has copies of all the house and outbuilding keys in there. Except ..."

"Except what?"

"He's away, and we need a key to get in the study, which he always keeps on him."

"Fine, we break the lock on the door then, can't be too hard," Adelaide replied. "A few good whacks with a hammer."

"If you two are right about them, going around hitting things with a hammer will not do you any favours," Charlie said. "I can pick the lock, have a look and have it locked back up in five minutes."

79

Evelyn bit her lip and nodded.

"That's a great idea, but I want you to break into the study. There might be something of interest in there, and I'll like to have the key permanently."

ᚠᚦ

Every Wednesday afternoon, Roskopf and McGowen walked down to the village. That made it a perfect time to get Charlie from the ward, to Bramwell's study, and back again. Lucy would still be asleep, and even if she wasn't, she was unlikely to come down from the attic room.

True to his word, Charlie picked the lock within a minute, and Evelyn slipped in to find the key.

"What do you think you'll find?" Charlie asked.

"Honestly, I don't know. In the cellar we found nothing. Maybe we'll find nothing again." Adelaide sighed. "The cold we felt was real, but what if the rest is in my head?"

Evelyn walked out of the study, key in hand. "Well, let's go find out."

ᚠᚦ

The room was perfectly ordinary.

A trellis with a robust growth of ivy upon it had been placed on the outside of the window, so that it let in only a dappling of sunlight upon the virgin white walls. The room even shared the marble floor of the hallway, except in this room, the high shine of the stone stopped to form a perfect circle of darkness in the middle of the room. Evelyn switched the electric light on. The black hole metamorphosed into a stone staircase leading into the bowels of the house.

Having hastily gathered some candles from the drawing room, Evelyn and Adelaide readied themselves for the descent into the unknown.

"I want to see what's down there," Charlie whined.

"Absolutely not," Adelaide intoned. "God knows how far down it goes. What if your legs gave way? Me and Evelyn aren't going to drag you back up."

"Addy, please," Charlie pleaded; Riley joined in with a whine, attempting to get his mistress's attention.

"No."

"Evelyn?"

"No." Evelyn said, struggling to keep a straight face.

"Fine, I'll keep watch then."

"You know it makes sense," Adelaide said.

"Riley, you stay here with Charlie."

Riley wagged his tail as he went to sit beside Charlie, who was now leaning against the door.

"Time's ticking, girls. You don't have long until they're back."

Evelyn lit the candles, handing one to Adelaide. "Ready when you are."

ᚹᚦ

The stone steps were worn smooth; they were far from being the first to traverse down into the depths.

"You're telling me you've lived here all your life, and you really never knew that there was a subterranean cave beneath your feet?" In the flickering light, Adelaide swore she saw a smirk play across Evelyn's features.

"That's something you'll have to let go of." Evelyn laughed before suddenly stopping to grasp at Adelaide's shoulder. "What's that?"

Adelaide looked towards where Evelyn tipped her candle. There was something embedded in the stone, reflecting the candle's light at the bottom of the steps.

"If I didn't know better, I'd say it was a piece of mirror."

They continued on down, before Evelyn said, "I think the ground has levelled off here."

Sure enough, Adelaide found that there were no longer any steps. The light from the candles cast long shadows across the wall. Shadows that looked very familiar to her. Shadows with long limbs that played and danced across the stone. So focused was she on the darkness' movements, Adelaide didn't notice the potholes on the floor. She tripped, managing, only just, to right herself. The candle fell to the ground.

"Jesus, are you okay?" Evelyn's voice echoed and reverberated around the cave.

"Yes, I'm fine, I don't know where that damn candle rolled off to, though."

Adelaide and Evelyn crouched, feeling for it, and Adelaide noticed that the stone beneath her fingertips repeated a pattern of whorls and Vs.

"Evelyn, bring the light closer."

Evelyn carefully dipped her candle down to the floor. Stone carvings littered the ground. Adelaide spied the errant candle. Grabbing it, she relit it with Evelyn's and stood. The light didn't reach the walls; they remained shrouded in inky curtains. She moved towards the darkness, the candle's light drawing back the veil.

The entire cave was filled with thousands of symbols.

CHAPTER TEN

Adelaide sat in silence as Evelyn told Charlie what they had found in the cave. A kernel of knowledge gnawed at the back of Adelaide's mind, trying to break its way to the fore.

"Witch marks," she muttered.

Evelyn and Charlie turned to her.

"What?" Charlie asked.

"We had a mark like the ones down there by our fireplace. A woman told us it was called a witch mark."

"So, they summon witches?" Charlie said hesitantly.

"No, they're meant to protect, to ward off evil. She told us they are common in old houses. Above doorways, chimneys, any entrances in which evil could enter. It always seemed quaint. Now I've seen all of them gathered in one place, it seems a little scary now."

"From how many you said are down there, it must be well and truly covered."

Adelaide walked over to Charlie's bedside.

"This," she held out the puzzle. Riley, thinking it was something for him to chew on, jumped up and tried to grab it. She lifted it out of reach. "These shapes are just like the ones down there."

"Do you think it protected us?" Charlie said. "Sounds mad, doesn't it?"

"It does." Adelaide handed it to him. "But maybe you should keep a hold of it, just in case."

Throughout this exchange, Evelyn had been deathly silent. What little colour she normally possessed had drained away. Adelaide embraced her, resting her forehead against Evelyn's cheek. She felt cool to the touch.

"What's the matter, darling?"

Evelyn looked at Adelaide, blue eyes wide.

"There's so many," she whispered. "What were they trying to keep trapped?"

ᚱ

After the twin events of Dugdale's death and the foray into the cave, Adelaide thought Evelyn would be more curious than ever about Ashthorne and its secrets. Instead, though, she seemed determined to ignore it all. Talking at length about her friends down south, how she'd like to get another dog, but was worried Riley would not take to having her attention split, anything and everything but the cave and its strange markings.

She seemed in many ways a different woman than the one Adelaide had seen arguing with passion earlier that day. Was this something she did, take everything and hide it in a locked box so that it would be easier to walk away from?

At the back of the courtyard stood a small a small outbuilding whose windows someone had bricked over. The mortar between those bricks was clean, free of the lichen that clung to the rest of the brickwork. The door, ancient and heavy with its dark green paint peeling away in great swaths, had been fitted a new bolt and padlock, the bright silver starkly contrasting with the rust-flecked hinges.

Often, Evelyn and Adelaide would sit watching Riley as he played in the courtyard. Occasionally, his ears would twitch as he watched the door intently, before padding up and scratching at it. He'd wait for a response until, receiving none, he'd lose interest and go back to playing.

Today he seemed more agitated than usual, pawing and whining.

"Riley, come away." He trotted over to Evelyn and looked up at her expectedly.

"What does he think is in there?" Adelaide asked.

"Rodents," said a woman's voice harshly. Justine's mother stood beside them clutching a stoneware dish wrapped in a tea towel. "They get everywhere."

She started towards the locked door, before stopping so abruptly that the dish's lid clattered. She turned on her heels and went back into the house

"Rather strange, don't you think?" Adelaide said,

"Most people are strange around here," Evelyn replied, scratching behind Riley's ears. "That's why I left as soon as I could."

That pang of worry hit Adelaide again. Would Evelyn just up and leave? Wake up one day filled with that urge to travel?

Evelyn grabbed Adelaide's hand, giving it a squeeze.

"What do you think is in there?"

"I've never really thought about it. Wood? Coal? Doesn't concern me."

Adelaide wondered, not for the first time, what growing up in Evelyn's world must have been like. Her family had always been comfortable, but money had been a point of contention between her parents. As her father had risen in status at work, so had his wife believed that it ought to be reflected in their social standing. She had married beneath her class for love and came to deeply regret it. What had she gained in the end? A dead son, and a daughter who may as well have been dead. Was it any wonder she had turned to barbiturates?

How could Evelyn be so free and blasé all the while? Did anything really matter to her? Was Bramwell right when he said that Evelyn hadn't the capacity for loyalty?

"You alright? You looked a bit far away there."

"I'm fine."

ᚠᚼ

Evelyn and Adelaide had passed the last ten minutes of the forty-minute walk into the village in an easy and companionable silence.

After their foray into the caves, Evelyn had reverted to the quiet reflection which characterised her troubled mind. When the next few days had passed without incident, she relaxed and, upon learning that Adelaide had the day free, suggested a trip into Advent.

The day, although brisk in temperature, was a fine one, and the walk had been pleasant and easy, with Adelaide asking questions about the village and its residents before they fell into silence.

They came to the church. All the windows had been replaced with clear glass. Adelaide would have dismissed it as a cost cutting measure, were it not for the lead shot through it. Lead arranged in the same geometric pattern as the mirror.

"Well, that's new," Evelyn said.

"Someone smashed all the windows in last month, I was passing through the village so went in to have a look. Justine was in there by herself clearing up, it was so strange; she started talking about how the place is rotten."

"Advent is hardly a model village," Evelyn said.

"I think she was including the house in that. Incidentally, she also gave me a warning about you."

"Well, if she's worried about me corrupting you, I think that ship has well and truly sailed."

Adelaide glanced around. Seeing no one in sight, she gave Evelyn the briefest of kisses before saying, "Do you think the same craftsman who made the windows also did the mirrors? They don't look as if they'd be cheap."

"The poor box was probably pilfered to pay for them," Evelyn muttered.

"I get the impression that you're not a fan of the local clergy."

Evelyn took a moment before answering.

"Edward Peters is nothing but a leach. There's a rumour that a girl who helped with the church upkeep was caught with child. She went to visit family in Yorkshire and came back alone. But she doesn't tend to the church anymore."

"That's reason enough not to like him. Nobody should abuse their power in that manner."

"That he's one of the few men left here makes it pretty obvious that he was the one responsible. A lot of the women, young and old, seem to fawn over him. I suppose it's only natural after losing someone close to them."

Adelaide thought of the way she had come to love and depend on Charlie so much. She knew that if they'd have been so lucky to have met under different circumstances they would have bonded, but the loss of her brother had added an extra dimension to it for Adelaide.

"That's not the only reason," Evelyn continued. "He's friends with Grayson Roskopf."

"The friend of my enemy is my enemy."

"It certainly makes him untrustworthy in my eyes. This is it," Evelyn said as they rounded the corner. "There isn't much, but there are a few small shops and a halfway decent tearoom."

"Sounds wonderful. I can't remember the last time someone made me a cup of tea."

The two women stood in the village courtyard before the well.

"What's this?" Adelaide asked, indicating the structure that surrounded the well. Written in white flowers pressed into a clay bed, was:

"Servants, be subject to your masters with all fear; not only to the good and gentle, but also to the froward."
1 Peter 2:18

"Is it the verse or the custom that eludes you?" a male voice asked.

"Reverend Edwards, I trust you are well," Evelyn said politely.

He was tall, approaching six feet in height. His dark hair was so closely cropped that his scalp showed through. He might have been handsome, had his features not been so sharp. The man needed sanding down.

Edward stepped past Evelyn, his eyes on Adelaide.

"This is a well dressing. It's a rather quaint custom unique to Derbyshire."

Adelaide was more than aware of this; that it was entirely the wrong time of year for a well-dressing was what irked her. Closer inspection revealed the flowers to be made of silk. The manmade materials, along with the use of the verse, made it so far removed from any well dressing she'd seen before as to be unrecognisable. The whole thing seemed more suited to a funeral than the celebration of spring.

"The verse reminds us we must endure suffering as Christ did, to willingly submit to every human authority for God's sake."

"So by the reasoning of this passage, we all should have submitted to the will of the Kaiser?" Adelaide said, her eyes firmly locking with those of the Vicar. "And by extension of that reasoning, my brother died for naught. Millions of men died for naught."

"That is a rather simplistic way of putting it."

"No more simplistic than the church itself." Out of the corner of her eye, Adelaide could see Evelyn discreetly try-ing to repress her laughter.

"If you'll excuse us, Miss Ashthorne and I have things to do."

Linking her arm through Evelyn's, Adelaide steered them past a horse-drawn cart loaded with rough-cut stone, towards the tearoom.

"I can't believe you said that to him," whispered Evelyn. "I don't think I'd ever dare."

"And here I was thinking you were a rebel."

They stopped outside a shop window full of Blue John jewellery and trinkets. The bands of purple and yellow fashioned into a knife handle, complete with mother-of-pearl blade, mesmerised Adelaide.

Evelyn moved closer until Adelaide could feel her breath against her neck.

"Do you like it?" Evelyn asked softly.

"It reminds me of you."

"Sharp and stony? How flattering."

"Beautiful, practical, an exquisite example of Derbyshire craftmanship. It's even in your colours." In the right light, Evelyn's blue eyes did take on a violet hue. Adelaide smiled at Evelyn's reflection in the window. How did I get so lucky? she thought, lost in her deep blue eyes. Then suddenly, Evelyn was no longer there, replaced by a void. She couldn't see anything but darkness; not even the shop's display was visible. From the corner of her eyes Adelaide saw the edges of the glass covered with white velvet frosting.

"Let's buy it!" Evelyn started for the shop door just as the quarry horse cart suddenly shifted and jerked forward. A large piece of sandstone broke from its rope moorings and fell to the ground, the noise causing the massive shire horse to rear up. Evelyn grabbed Adelaide's coat and pulled her violently back, just as the horse's hoofs came crashing down, sickeningly close to where Adelaide's head had been.

"Oh God." Evelyn wrapped her arms around Adelaide "Are you alright?"

"Yes, I'm just not sure what happened."

By then, the cart's driver, hearing the commotion, had rushed out of the pub, and was apologising profusely.

"I think we should go home," Evelyn said. Adelaide nodded silently in agreement.

ᛦ

Adelaide clutched the warm cup of tea, which Evelyn had insisted upon lacing with brandy.

"How is it?" Evelyn asked, sitting down beside her.

"Disgusting. I don't think I'll ever learn to like brandy." She took Evelyn's hand. "But thank you."

"I love you."

"Really."

"That's not the response I was hoping for." A small smile tugged at the corners of her lips. "But yes, I do. Thinking that horse could have hurt you, or that I might lose you, made me realise it."

"I love you, too."

"I still don't understand why that horse startled the way she did." Evelyn had that same contemplative look she'd worn when she had wondered what could possibly warrant the witch marks down in the cave.

"I was sporting blasphemy, maybe it was divine retribution," Adelaide said, squeezing Evelyn's hand.

"You're teasing me."

"It was an accident."

Evelyn fell quiet.

"Evelyn, it was an accident. Nothing more."

CHAPTER ELEVEN

"Aren't you curious to see what else might be down there?" Adelaide asked Evelyn. Charlie had talked incessantly about the cave of late, obsessed with the mystery of it all, and had been begging her to go back down to have another look. It seemed as if Charlie's curiosity was infectious.

Evelyn looked at Adelaide with an expression that said, *are you serious?*

"There can't really be anything down there?" Adelaide continued. "Can there?"

"I don't think we should tempt it; we've had one death. Leave it be."

Adelaide nodded in agreement, but she was disappointed. It wasn't just Charlie's enthusiasm that drove her, it was a need to know that she wasn't losing her mind. That no matter if the explanation was natural or supernatural, there was an explanation.

"I got you a present." Evelyn reached over Adelaide and picked up a box from the bedside table. "Here."

Adelaide opened it, revealing the Blue John and pearl knife.

"I wanted us to have a memento of that day. I keep thinking that maybe it protected you. If you hadn't been standing in that exact spot admiring it—I know that if anything happened to you ..." Evelyn faltered here. "That's why I like you safe in bed every night," she drew Adelaide closer, "amongst other things."

As the fire died down, and Evelyn's breathing slowed into the soft rhythm of sleep, Adelaide watched the shadow on the wall, pulling Evelyn close to her in an effort to fight off the impeding chill.

ᚠᚦ

"I think Evelyn's in danger," Adelaide whispered to Charlie. "The shadow I keep seeing ... it's as though it's edging its way closer to her all the while. That night it froze my hand—what if it was trying to keep me from her?"

Charlie's eye widened with excitement. "We're going down?"

"We're going down," Adelaide confirmed. "I don't know if we'll find an answer—"

"We'll find something," Charlie said.

"I don't know what I'm more afraid of, finding something, or not. Charlie?"

"Un-huh," he said absently.

"There aren't just those marks down there, there's something else ..."

"Yes?" Charlie said, a little more attentively now.

"I think there's a piece of mirror down there, it makes me wonder ..."

"Yes?" he said, still ever patient.

"Sounds crazy, but I thought they might be a connection and if there is—"

"When do we go?" Charlie said, ignoring Adelaide's worries.

"This afternoon. McGowen and Roskopf are out of the house."

Charlie beamed. The whole thing seemed to be nothing more than a scouting expedition, and Adelaide said as much to him.

"You can be a Girl Guide then."

"Can't say I'm enthused with the uniform."

"I think you'd rather suit a flouncy blouse and tie. My sister used to wear bright scarlet, but that would clash with your hair. Blue or green would suit you better."

"No," Adelaide said firmly.

47

Once again, Adelaide stood at the cave's mouth, looking into the abyss.

"Are you alright?" Charlie stood beside her, looking slightly apprehensive.

"Fine," Adelaide let out a slight chuckle, "you?"

"Fine, not about to shit myself with terror at all," Charlie turned to Adelaide. "Ladies first, then."

She stepped down, the heavy thud of Charlie's false leg on the stone behind her. It took a little longer to reach the plateau with Charlie than it did with Evelyn.

"It's not as bad as I thought it'd be."

"What did you expect, blood dripping from the walls?"

Charlie lifted his lantern. "No, but I thought there'd be more of these marks. I think 'greatly exaggerated' is the phrase I'm looking for." Charlie moved forward. "I think you were right about the mirror. I don't know how it could be possible, but it's as if the stone has formed around it." Charlie brushed his finger over the surface.

"No, this can't be," Adelaide looked around the cave. Where before the witch marks had numbered in the hundreds, there now remained about three dozen. "I swear to god when me and Evelyn—"

A bone-crunching thud interrupted her; Charlie had hit the floor and now lay twitching.

"Charlie?"

Adelaide dropped to her knees beside him.

"Charlie!" She turned him onto his side. Spittle bubbled at his mouth as his legs kicked out futilely, trying to carry him away. His eye was wide open but glazed over, no longer seeing her.

Adelaide didn't dare leave to get help. What if he choked to death whilst she was gone? She couldn't even call for help. Screaming at the top of her lungs would only bounce the sound around them, enveloping them, but not carrying it out of the cave's mouth. Panic griped Adelaide's heart like a vice, each second a turn of the handle, squeezing it tighter.

I should have listened, she thought. *If I'd listened, we'd be upstairs playing cards right now and he'd be fine.*

Just as she thought all hope was lost, Charlie's legs stilled, his eyes refocused, and he wiped the spittle from his mouth.

"Addy, what's the matter?"

"Charlie, you bastard." Tears streamed down Adelaide's cheeks. "I thought you were dying."

"I don't know what happened. I remember feeling faint and a bit dizzy, then next thing I know you're kneeling beside me blubbering like an idiot." Charlie smiled, letting Adelaide know his words were in jest. "I suppose I'm out of condition, and those steps took it out of me more than I thought they would."

Adelaide swallowed, the painful lump in her throat not going away.

"Are you sure you're okay?" Her voice was a hoarse whisper.

"I'm fine."

It struck Adelaide that the conversation they were having was eerily similar to the one she and Evelyn had the night her hand suffered the frostnip.

"Help me up, won't you?"

Adelaide got to her feet and extended a hand to Charlie, helping him clamber awkwardly to his feet. They left the cave without noticing that the spittle on the floor had turned to ice.

ᚠᚦ

Adelaide and Riley had begun a habit of walking into the village every evening while Evelyn had dinner with her father.

As they reached the church, she saw the glow of light coming from within.

Curious, she changed their normal route and made a bee-line for the gate, but once they reached it, Riley gave a small whine and would go no further.

"It's okay, boy. You can stay here. I just want to see what's going on in here."

She walked up the path. Edward's voice boomed out from beyond the heavy doors. Edging closer, she saw the door was open a fraction. She opened it a fraction more and slipped through.

The place was no longer a place of worship for a Christian god. All traces of the Church of England had been erased. No cross adorned the walls. They had cut the pews back, so that they were little more than benches, all packed. Adelaide had never seen a church so full before.

How could it be, Adelaide thought, that it was colder in here than outside?

Despite all the bodies packed within, frost hung in the air.

Edward stood at what was once the pulpit. The glass window behind him reflected his congregation.

"This war may be over, but it won't be long until the next one. Will we satisfy them with only sons next time? No, they will come for your daughters, too."

A murmur of agreement moved through Edward's audience like a wave. As she looked around at the ardent, fevered faces, she noticed the overwhelming majority were female. Mrs Lennox was amongst them; no Justine though. The few men scattered throughout were old, too old for war.

"Which is why we must work to prevent this from happening again. Our village has been luckier than most. We have prospered, whilst others around us have failed. People flock to us. The Blue John stone is plentiful and tourists flock to buy it. They come to take the waters, stay in our inns. This is thanks to Her. She has protected us, but the time has come to give back—"

His eyes locked on Adelaide's.

"Miss Frost." His eyebrows raised as his lips curled into a sardonic smile. "So glad you're able to join us this evening. No Miss Ashthorne, though?"

The entire village turned to look at Adelaide, her heart rising in response. She'd been looked upon with disdain before, but never by a hundred eyes at once.

Adelaide turned and ran, the sound of Edward's laughter following her.

CHAPTER TWELVE

All the journey home Riley seemed uneasy. As they walked up the driveway, he broke free from Adelaide's admittedly loose grip and bounded up the side of the house.

Adelaide gave chase. He was heading towards the conservatory.

Once Riley reached the door, rather than patiently wait for Adelaide to catch up as he normally did, he pawed and whined. The click of his claws against the glass sounded a staccato in the night air.

"Fine," she called. "Seeing as how we're here now, we may as well get out of the wind a bit."

Reaching the door, she let him in, expecting him to go straight to his bed by the stove. Instead, he lingered by the doorway, licking at the flagstone before plonking down, splaying his back legs out in order to press himself as close to the cold ground as possible.

He was still softly whining to himself as Adelaide crouched down to stroke him. "Are you not feeling well, little man?"

She put her hand on the floor to steady herself as she got up. She had expected the stone to be smooth, but she felt a familiar pattern of whorls and triangles.

Despite Riley's best efforts to make himself a dead weight, Adelaide easily shifted him to the side. The same marks that littered the cave adorned the stone beneath him. He scrambled to lay himself back on the marks.

"Come on, let's get you back to the house. Evelyn will be missing you." She tugged gently on his lead, but he held steadfast.

"We've got to go." Riley still refused to budge. "Fine, if you're going to be awkward, I can just leave you here." Adelaide was halfway out the door before letting out a sigh, turning around and picking him up. "She's spoilt you."

Riley looked up and licked Adelaide's cheek.

"Yes, spoiled."

ᚠᚣ

"Charlie?" The question was a whisper in the dark. Charlie shifted in an effort to get up, and Adelaide resisted the urge to help him, not wanting to contribute to his feeling of help-lessness. She waited patiently until he was sitting upright.

"How did you cope over there? With being scared?"

"Me? Nah, I were never scared."

Adelaide had come to think of Charlie as a younger brother in their time together, but it made her heart ache now, as she realised he really had only just become a man. He had been no more than a boy when he had been sent away to fight.

"I cried a lot in the early days, but after a while, after that feeling of constant fear seeps into your bones, your flesh, and dulls to anxiety, you end up not feeling much of anything. There's no room for it."

Adelaide considered this for a moment. Was this why Justine was closed off?

"Has Justine ever spoken to you about the village?"

"You mean has she ever spoken about the vicar and the church?"

"Yes."

"Justine is a woman of true Christian faith and so was soon ousted by this new congregation. This new bloke just turned up one day; there was no indication that the previous vicar was to be replaced. He was at his pulpit one day, then simply gone the next. All they have is the word of this Peters fella that he was the representative of the parish. Her mother was taken in quite quickly by him, and the rest of the village soon followed suit. It's no longer a Christian church."

"I was there last night, the atmosphere in that place—it was like just before a summer storm, as if lightning could strike at any moment. And it was so cold, so bloody cold. Riley wouldn't go near the place."

"I'd trust the dog on this one Addy, he's extremely smart, had me clocked as a good 'un straight away."

"I think you're right. When we came back to the house, he made a bolt for the conservatory. There's a flagstone there that I just couldn't get him to budge from. It had markings on it."

"Like the ones in the cellar?"

Adelaide nodded.

"What do you think it means?" Charlie asked.

"I don't know, but it scares me."

"Leave—you and Evelyn. Just go, nothing else is keeping you here."

Even if Evelyn would agree to leave, how could she ever leave Charlie behind? Adelaide doubted that Justine, despite her wish to leave the village, would agree to leave together, and Charlie would never leave without Justine. So here they all were, stuck in this house.

CHAPTER THIRTEEN

Adelaide walked onto the ward one morning to find Edward deep in conversation with McGowen; she'd heard snippets drifting down the hall.

"Bramwell …"

"Liability …"

But as soon as the vicar spotted Adelaide, he broke off his talk with McGowen and strode towards her.

"Miss Frost." He grabbed both of Adelaide's hands in his. "I'm so glad to see you are well. I saw that business with the Shire horse. That must have been an awful fright for you, my dear."

Why was he pretending that that day in the village was the last time they had met?

Adelaide pulled her hands sharply away. "Accidents happen, Reverend."

"That they do, that they do." A sardonic smile twitched at the corners of his mouth. "Elizabeth was telling me about the wonderful work you do here. You must feel so proud to work for such a brilliant woman."

"I have work to be getting on with," Adelaide said coolly.

"Yes, of course, Miss Frost." He turned back to McGowen. "I shall be seeing you again soon, Elizabeth, and of course, I'll check in on Bramwell." He regarded Adelaide with appreciative eyes. "Goodbye Miss Frost. I'm sure I'll see you soon as well."

He stalked out of the ward, leaving Adelaide to wonder why they had been discussing Evelyn's father.

Ten minutes after Edward left, Adelaide made an excuse to leave the ward. She hadn't heard the front door, so he had to still be in the house. Slipping off her shoes, Adelaide quietly padded along the hallway until she stood outside Mr Ashthorne's study.

"I understand you may have reservations, but I can assure you that this is all for the greater good, and you are fulfilling your part of her work admirably." Edward, so used to speaking from the pulpit, made no attempt to mute his words.

"You're right, of course."

"It's quite all right. Everyone experiences a crisis of faith at one time or another. How it's handled and overcome is what matters in the eyes of the lord."

"I miss her so much," Bramwell said, his voice so low Adelaide struggled to hear him.

"Your sacrifice will be but a temporary one, Bramwell." She heard a chair being pushed back, followed by footsteps. She quickly retreated in search of Evelyn.

Adelaide told Evelyn what she had overheard.

"I'm going to ask him what he meant by 'temporary sacrifice'," Evelyn said.

"Evelyn, no."

"Don't worry. I'll say that I was the one outside the door."

"That's not what I'm worried about," Adelaide called, as Evelyn rushed off. Riley bounded behind her, thinking that this was a great game in which his participation was vital.

She was through the front door by the time Adelaide reached the bottom of the hall steps.

It was at the fountain that she caught up with her and Edward. Evelyn stood in front of him.

"I need to ask you what you meant when you told my father that the sacrifice was only temporary." Evelyn was calm and collected, her words conveying only a mild curiosity.

Edward's face contorted into that snarling, sardonic smile. "All things on this earth are fleeting until we enter the kingdom of heaven," he said. "Goodbye, Miss Ashthorne."

He turned to face Adelaide. "Your friend would do well to learn not to continually question my authority."

Adelaide glanced at Evelyn, who stood fists and jaw clenched, looking for all the world like she'd strike him down if she could.

Getting into his car, he added, "You should come for a drive with me one afternoon. I could show you some wondrous sights."

With this, he slammed the car door and started the engine, kicking up the gravel as he drove away.

ᚠᚦ

Adelaide followed Evelyn back into the house, thinking maybe she shouldn't have told Evelyn about this at all. This, and what had transpired in the church last night, had only moved Evelyn's fixation from Roskopf to Edward. Adelaide had concluded that Roskopf was irrelevant. McGowen ran the show here, and the personal relationship she had with Edward was disturbing.

She hadn't time to discuss this further with Evelyn, though, as McGowen collared her, telling her to get back to work. It wasn't long after that McGowen excused herself, leaving Adelaide alone.

"Addy," Charlie called. "Can you help me with something?"

"Anything."

Charlie smiled.

ᚠᚦ

"What's this about?" Justine asked, as Adelaide led her through the house.

"It's a surprise."

"I know Charlie told me to trust you—"

"And you'll see that he was right." Adelaide opened the door to the sunroom.

Bathed in the glow of the candles which lined the room stood Charlie, his olive drab uniform pressed and hair neatly combed; he held a bunch of flowers, a smile on his marred face.

The Victrola played softly as Charlie offered his hand to Justine. "May I please have this dance?"

For this moment, they were simply a man and a woman sharing a dance, no war, no sickness.

Adelaide quietly left.

CHAPTER FOURTEEN

"I can drive."

Evelyn's words wrenched Adelaide back from the brink of sleep. She rolled over to face her.

"And?" she said, trailing her fingers down Evelyn's side.

"I was running it over in my head. If I had a car of my own, I could take you places."

"If you want to show me wondrous sights, I see two every time you take your clothes off," Adelaide said, before capturing Evelyn in a kiss.

Evelyn yielded to Adelaide before pulling away to say, "Don't you think he sounded smug, asking you to go for a drive with him?"

"Miss Ashthorne, I do believe you're jealous."

"No! Okay—maybe I am—just a little."

"I'd never get in that car. You know that."

115

"I know. I find it frustrating not being able to tell him off for making advances towards you. If I were a man—"

"If you were a man, I wouldn't be in your bed."

"I wish I could have told my mother about you. I wish I could tell everyone about you."

"What would you tell them?"

Adelaide climbed atop Evelyn, straddling her hips, looking down at her silvery blonde hair spread across the pillows, the delicate rise and fall of her chest as she looked up at her.

"I'd tell them I've met that my soulmate and if it was at all possible, I'd ask her to marry me," Evelyn said.

"Wait, what?"

"Why are you surprised? I've told you multiple times that I love you more than anything."

"I love you too."

Adelaide bent down, planting a soft kiss on Evelyn's lips, before moving to her neck. Rewarded with a moan, she moved lower to Evelyn's breasts, taking one nipple into her mouth while brushing her thumb lightly over the other. Evelyn arched her back in response.

Adelaide continued her way down, lingering on her stomach, infuriating Evelyn to the point that she buried her fingers in her hair and attempted to push her further down.

"Don't rush me," she murmured, moving to Evelyn's inner thighs and placing the lightest of kisses on them.

"Please," Evelyn breathed.

Suppressing a giggle, Adelaide moved her tongue over Evelyn's centre. Evelyn gasped as Adelaide continued her ministrations, entwining her fingers into Adelaide's hair pulling at it with every stroke of Adelaide's tongue.

Spurred on, Adelaide quickened her rhythm. Sensing she was near, she slipped two fingers in; curling them just so, she pushed Evelyn over the edge.

Evelyn let out a cry just as another, shriller, scream filled the air.

Adelaide made her way back up Evelyn, and was nuzzling into the hollow of her throat when the scream sounded again.

"What was that?" Adelaide leapt from the bed, trying to gather her clothes together. "Sounds like it came from the ward."

Evelyn moved to sit on the edge of the bed. The scream sounded again.

Adelaide put her ear to Evelyn's door. "It sounds like Lucy," she said, undoing the bolt and stepping through the door.

ᚠᚦ

In the hallway, Adelaide could hear McGowen and Roskopf talking.

"The girl's being hysterical. I knew she had no strength of character. A little blood and reduced to this," McGowen said.

Adelaide debated wherever to carry on down the hall to the ward. It would be obvious that the only place she could have come from was Evelyn's bedroom. And in her night clothes, no less. It'd take only a second for McGowen's suspicions to become resolute fact.

The decision to reveal herself was quickly taken out of her hands when Evelyn walked past her, straight towards Roskopf.

"What's going on?"

Adelaide marvelled. Even in a nightgown with her hair dishevelled, Evelyn maintained every ounce of poise and grace. They didn't look at Evelyn, their focus on Lucy who stood shaking.

"If nether of you are prepared to answer a simple question, then we'll look for ourselves. Adelaide?"

Heat rose to Adelaide's cheeks as she stepped from the shadows. McGowen's eyes flitted from Adelaide to Evelyn and back again with a knowing smirk.

"I'll leave you to deal with this," Roskopf said to McGowen. He looked pale and gaunt, a sheen of sweat on his brow. Whatever had happened, he was distressed by it greatly. He walked away, looking rather broken.

Evelyn took Lucy in her arms. "It's alright now. Whatever it is, it can't be all that bad."

Lucy's sobbing died down into intermittent gasps.

"It's everywhere. I'd never seen so much at once."

"Seen so much what?" Evelyn asked. Adelaide didn't wait for Lucy's answer, she already knew. She took a deep breath, stealing herself as she stepped onto the ward.

Adelaide had expected the blood, but like Lucy had said, she'd never seen so much of it at once.

Charlie lay dead in his bed. Moving closer, Adelaide saw the blue ceramic fragments of a water jug littering the bed and floor.

Charlie's stomach had been slashed multiple times, each cut a starting point for his skin to have been pared back like ribbons. The wounds were bloodless, showing as stripes of yellow fat. His hand still gripped a vicious looking shard, its raw edge spotted with blood.

How long had Charlie spent silently mutilating himself until his body gave up?

Amongst the blood and confusion, Adelaide noticed the wooden puzzle was gone.

She strode out of the ward. Her stomach tight, the burn of bile biting at the back of her throat. No, Charlie wouldn't do this! Mere hours ago he had danced with Justine. He was happy. He had a future.

Lucy was still shivering in Evelyn's arms.

"Where were you?" Adelaide clutched Lucy by the shoulders, wrenching her away from Evelyn, forcing her to face her.

"I was at the desk the whole time."

"And you noticed nothing?" Adelaide pushed Lucy away. She stumbled, almost falling, before regaining her balance. Adelaide saw McGowen watching with what could only be described as amusement.

"Adelaide, it happened so quickly."

"You can't blame Lucy." This from Evelyn. But Adelaide was unwilling to listen to excuses.

"It wasn't quick, it was slow and deliberate." She spat the words, letting rage fill her so there would be no space for pain.

Lucy mumbled something

"Excuse me?"

"I may have been asleep," Lucy whispered.

"What?"

"I was asleep," Lucy sobbed. "I don't know how it happened. I was drinking my tea and then nothing. When I opened my eyes, there was blood everywhere."

"You're of no use to us tonight. You may as well sleep off the hysterias." McGowen took Lucy by the shoulder and steered her away. She took a few steps and then turned back to say. "I have to say Adelaide, I've always pegged you as the more level-headed one, despite your unnatural tendencies."

"Do you think the cup's still there?" Evelyn asked, when they were alone. Adelaide immediately guessed her train of thought. Someone had drugged Lucy. She followed Evelyn to the desk; a cup, still half full, sat there. Evelyn picked it up and brought it to her nose.

"You won't smell anything, it's odourless."

Evelyn dipped her finger in the remaining liquid and tasted it. "It's bitter."

"It's Veronal." Adelaide took the cup. "We use it when the men need calming down, or if they have trouble sleeping."

"So, Lucy could have dosed her own drink?"

"No, McGowen is the only one who has a key," Adelaide said, still bristling with anger. "We've always assumed that they were taking the men down to the cellar for their sessions. What if they've been going down into the cave? When me and Charlie went down—"

"You went down there again? With Charlie?"

"He experienced something in that cave. It's my fault. I took him down there and now he's dead, and it's my fault."

Evelyn took her into her arms. "You can't blame yourself."

"You didn't see him." Adelaide tried to disentangle herself from Evelyn's arms but was held fast. "The way he was writhing on that floor, foaming at the mouth. Maybe it did break something in him? I should have known, I should have protected him."

"It wasn't your fault," Evelyn said.

The tears threatened to flow, but there was something she had to do first.

"We need to tell Justine."

CHAPTER FIFTEEN

The body was gone; the blood remained.

"You're here." McGowen held a mop in her hand, which she forcibly shoved towards Adelaide. "Clean this up."

Adelaide dutifully mopped the blood from the floor and stripped the sheets, which were red and tacky in their centre, brown and crisp at the edges where the blood had fully dried. The thin mattress was soaked through. Adelaide doubted it was worth saving, but nevertheless dragged it outside for Justine's mother to attempt to wash clean.

Personally, she'd take a match to the thing. It wasn't worth saving.

She rested a moment after finally managing to place the mattress in the rear courtyard outside the kitchen. She knew from experience that the mattresses were not especially heavy, but it was weighted down now by Charlie's life.

Adelaide's entire body ached; her eyes burned from lack of sleep. Evelyn had driven her to the house Justine and her mother shared; she couldn't let Justine come to the house, to risk her seeing Charlie or the carnage left behind. She couldn't let her be told by McGowen in her customary vile manner what Charlie had done to himself.

Justine did all the things Adelaide wished she could. She had screamed, thrown things, most notably a pair of ceramic horses that shattered against the door frame, all the while her tears flowing without shame. Once Justine had exhausted herself, she fell into a fretful sleep, punctuated with chest racking sobs. Only then did Adelaide and Evelyn leave.

On their way back to the house, Evelyn said, "I hate to ask, but—"

"But what?"

"McGowen respected you last night when you didn't break down when you saw—when you saw—"

"My friend bloodied, mutilated, and dead?"

"I think she may open up to you, if you played it right, of course."

"What do you mean?"

"Be cold, detached. Hell, denounce me if you have to!"

A soft scraping, as if fingernails were being racked across velvet, jolted Adelaide back to the now. It was coming from the outbuilding. She pressed her ear against the door, recoiling as a sharp piece of peeling paint stabbed her cheek. She plucked the offending article from the wood and stepped closer again. The noise was rhythmic: three long scratches, a pause, repeat. Adelaide didn't know how long she spent at the door before she heard hard-soled shoes on stone emanating from behind. She turned to see McGowen marching towards her.

Oh, fuck!

"I admire how you've got on with the job, no complaining. To be fair to you, Adelaide, I don't think I've ever heard you moan or whine about any aspect of your work. And unlike Lucy, you've never been stupid enough to be caught with child and thrown from the family home. I sincerely thought that with Charlie dead you would have left. Obviously, the tie that binds you here is stronger," McGowen's eyes were alive with interest. "Which brings us to your personal life—"

"My personal life is just that, personal."

"Your friendship with Miss Ashthorne?"

"It's not a friendship. She fulfils a function." Adelaide felt the rush of blood to her head; she could cope with the blood and gore, but disrespecting Evelyn made her sick to her stomach. Adelaide wasn't so stupid to think McGowen would suddenly approve of the fact that she preferred women to men, but Adelaide could already sense the shift in McGowen's attitude towards her.

"I'd like to talk in private, come to my room tonight." McGowen said.

"I'm flattered, but I think you're a little old for me." Adelaide was horrified at her own glibness. Had she gone too far? She hoped she'd been able to keep the neutral expression on her face.

"Your attempts at humour are not appreciated," McGowen said.

Adelaide nodded. Being with Evelyn had given her a confidence and sense of self that had been lacking before she came to Ashthorne. Her newfound verboseness would have to be kept in check if she were to ingratiate herself with Roskopf and McGowen.

"Tonight, Adelaide, we have much to discuss."

᛭

Adelaide continued to stare at the sink's bottom long after the water had run clear. She gripped the basin and, no longer able to hold back, let out a chest racking sob that turned into a series of them, before morphing into a scream.

In time, her breathing slowed, and the tears stopped flowing. Adelaide turned to face the day. Justine's mother, Mrs Lennox, was at the table peeling vegetables. She worked so silently, Adelaide was afraid to ask how long she had been there.

"No bread today," she said, throwing another potato into a bowl already overflowing with them. "No point even trying to make it."

"What?"

"No point," she carried on, as if Adelaide hadn't spoken. "Dough won't rise with a dead body in the house."

"How is Justine?" Adelaide asked tentatively, readying herself for Mrs Lennox to carry on with her tirade.

"It's a loss, to be sure, but what kind of future would she have had with the lad? Better for it to be over now, than later. I know she wants to leave, but the girl is better off here amongst her own kind."

Adelaide wondered how she could be so detached from Justine's anguish. During the night, whilst her daughter had sobbed, she had done nothing more than place a solitary cup of tea in front of Adelaide and gone to her own bed.

"Give her a day or two and she'll be right as rain."

"I don't think she will be."

Mrs Lennox met Adelaide with a stony glare; a look that said, *do you dare to say you know my own daughter better than me?* She placed her knife down by the unpeeled veg as the silence permeated the room. Adelaide left the kitchen, acutely aware of her eyes on the back of her neck.

ᚠᚦ

Adelaide wanted to find Evelyn, to tell her that McGowen was on the verge of letting her into the inner circle. This, however, wouldn't have been wise. She worked until it was time for her dinner break, then, bucking the norm of her and Evelyn eating together in the sunroom, she went looking for Lucy. Adelaide found her sitting on her bed fully dressed. In her hands was a silver locket, which she fidgeted with by opening and closing it repeatedly. Adelaide sat down beside her.

"How are you feeling?"

"Better, thank you. McGowen was right. I acted hysterically. What good would I have been in a field hospital, with men being mutilated by the shells and artillery daily? As much as I'd have tried to cope, I'd have been a hindrance."

Lucy put the locket down beside her, turning to face Adelaide for the first time. "It was inevitable, though."

"What was?" Adelaide asked.

"That one of them would kill themselves. What have they to live for? No woman would want them."

Had it been anyone but Charlie, Adelaide might have found herself unable to argue; it wasn't just the physical deformities—she would have liked to think some woman could see beyond looks—it was the complete decimation of their souls, but not Charlie's; he'd been a flame in the darkness.

"Justine loved him. I loved him and there are easier fucking ways to go than skinning yourself alive." Saying it aloud, it settled into Adelaide's mind that Charlie couldn't possibly have done that to himself. No matter what the evidence pointed to.

Lucy's eyes widened like a rabbit caught in a snare.

"You need to be careful, you and Evelyn both," she said, her panic rising; the wire tightening around her neck.

"Don't worry about us," Adelaide said bitterly.

"You may think you're being clever, but you're not!" Lucy was slipping towards hysteria again. Adelaide wondered if this was her natural state, and if McGowen had been sedating her since her arrival at Ashthorne.

"This is why I've come to talk with you. Help us prove that what they do causes more harm to those men—Charlie—after all they fought for. Giving their life to our King and country. We have a duty to protect them." Adelaide grasped Lucy's hands, facing her to look her in the eyes as she spoke. "Please, Lucy?"

Lucy pulled her hands away.

"No."

"No?"

"I'm leaving at the first opportunity."

"You can't, we need you."

"Why?"

Adelaide thought. Why did they need Lucy? She had fallen out of Roskopf's and McGowen's favour remarkably quickly. Was it the reassurance that came from knowing Lucy could bear witness to Roskopf's and McGowen's crimes? Or was it because she wanted to see Lucy punished?

"You can't think of a reason," Lucy said.

"You have nowhere to go, Lucy. Your father won't have you back," Adelaide said, recalling what McGowen told her in the courtyard. She knew it was a cruel blow to deal, yet she continued. "And what about money? Have you enough to last until you find a place to live and a job? If you stay—

help—Evelyn would make sure that you could have a room here as long as you need."

Lucy blinked blankly.

"Money! Evelyn and I could give you money enough to make a fresh start."

Lucy cast her eyes down to the floor as she gave an almost imperceptible nod of the head.

"No, I don't care anymore. Nothing is worth staying here."

ᚠᛈ

"Why have you been avoiding me?" Evelyn said, as she dragged Adelaide into the solarium. She mock scowled at Adelaide before, no longer able to keep up the charade, kissing her.

"This was your idea." Adelaide pulled Evelyn closer. "McGowen wants to speak to me tonight. I had to tell her you mean nothing to me. Lucy's leaving, but we don't need her."

"Adelaide, I was wrong to ask you to do this so soon after Charlie."

"It's because of him I want to do this."

The sound of footsteps emanated from the hallway. Adelaide and Evelyn quickly broke apart. Adelaide took three steps backwards to ensure that they were a respectable distance apart when Bramwell Ashthorne entered the room.

"Evelyn, I've been looking all over the house for you." He noticed Adelaide. "Miss Frost, I trust you are keeping well?"

"Yes sir, very well, thank you."

"Good. I need to speak with Evelyn privately, if you would be so kind." He made a motion with his hands, indicating that she should leave.

"Of course. Mr Ashthorne. Miss Ashthorne."

Adelaide exited the room, closing the door behind her. She stamped loudly down the hall before slipping her shoes off and tiptoeing back to the door. Adelaide pressed her ear against the wood.

"Promise me you won't be bringing shame on this house yet again." Bramwell's voice weighed heavily with weariness.

"You know I've never felt shame for who I am. My mother taught me that."

"Edward and I have been talking."

"About mother?"

"About you. He is willing to look past your indiscretions, which many men wouldn't." Bramwell said.

"No," Evelyn shouted.

"You could have a family, children of your own. I won't be here forever, and I don't want you dying alone as a spinster."

"Me not marrying does not equal my dying alone."

"I am your father. If you insist on staying on this course, you will have nothing from me. This house, the money, you will have none of it," Bramwell bellowed.

Adelaide had never heard him express anger before, or any potent emotion. He was a strangely dispassionate man. She felt sure that Bramwell would back down. Evelyn had told her how she'd always had her mother's support, and how much Bramwell adored his wife. Would he ignore her wish that he should never force Evelyn to go against her nature? More so, would Evelyn, scared by possible destitution, give in and submit?

"I'll talk to you once you've calmed down." The door swung open, leaving Adelaide face to face with Bramwell. "I don't blame you," he said.

She spluttered, searching for words to counteract him, but Bramwell pressed on. "You're not the first girl she's corrupted."

ASHTHORNE

He cast a steel-stony stare over his shoulder towards
Evelyn. "And you shouldn't kid yourself that you will be
the last. Evelyn hasn't the capacity for loyalty."

134

CHAPTER SIXTEEN

"We're going to leave. Take the car and leave. No matter
what he says, he's not going to set the constabulary on me."
Evelyn's voice rose in volume with each word.

There was a knock on the door, followed immediately
by Mrs Lennox opening it. "Your father is expecting you
for dinner."

Evelyn looked towards Adelaide.

"Go," Adelaide said.

Evelyn turned towards Mrs Lennox. "Just give me a minute."

Mrs Lennox left the room in a huff, muttering about not
being paid to be a messenger.

"You can't get the staff nowadays," Adelaide said, moving closer to Evelyn. "Go have dinner with your dad. Once
you're done, we'll work out what we're going to do and

where we'll go." She went to open the door for Evelyn, to see Mrs Lennox scurrying down the hall.

The early morning light creeped across the Peaks as Adelaide, Evelyn, and Riley made their way down to the converted stable that held the Ashthorne's motor car. Adelaide had only the carpet bag she came with; Evelyn, whose wardrobe was ten times that of Adelaide's, had been surprisingly economical and had filled only two bags, including several items she felt would suit Adelaide. A show of practicality that endeared her even more to Adelaide.

At the bottom of one bag, hidden beneath the clothes, was a stash of jewellery that had once belonged to Evelyn's mother, who, Evelyn felt certain, would not have minded it being sold should it need to be.

They had walked on stockinged feet through the house, going out via the kitchen. Justine and Mrs Lennox were not due for another two hours.

"You'll have to close the doors behind me. If we leave it open, father will know straight away we've taken the car."

Something felt off to Adelaide but it wasn't until Evelyn opened the stable doors that she realised what was bothering her. The latch had already been off the hook.

McGowen stood waiting, tangled in a cocoon of inertia. She blinked rapidly before the rest of her body sprang back to life. Riley growled.

"You've no right to stop us." Evelyn barged past her. "You had better move. I won't be held responsible when you get a foot run over." Riley's growl grew to a bark.

"I've not come to stop you, but I have information that may change your mind," McGowen said.

"Nothing you can say will change our minds." Adelaide moved closer to Evelyn, placing a hand on her shoulder. "I'd have thought you'd be glad to get rid of us. You'll be free to burrow further into Bramwell's ear."

"Your mother." McGowen said.

"What about her?" Evelyn said, eyes boring into McGowen.

"She didn't die. Your father lied to you."

Riley's long held suspicions were vindicated when McGowen led them to the outbuilding and produced a key for the lock. The inside had been made surprisingly opulent. Plush carpet and heavy tapestries lent a warmth despite the biting air outside.

"Family reunions should be a private matter," she sneered. "I'll leave you three alone."

ᚠᛈ

The outbuilding in which Evelyn's mother had been stowed away was more comfortable than the house itself. Plush carpet, the walls painted cornflower blue. There was even a radiator that Adelaide had found herself looking at with something approaching envy, remembering all those cold nights before she had found her way to Evelyn's bed.

Seeing the two of them together, it had never been clearer that Evelyn was very much her father's daughter. Whereas Evelyn was sharp of features and fair of hair, Mary had chestnut hair and a complexion that, although deprived of sun, still held the memory of it. There was a softness to her everywhere but her eyes. Her eyes held none of the intelligence and warmth that Evelyn had spoken of; they were as flat and dull as an old one penny coin. Mary Ashthorne took breath. She slept, water and food passed through her lips, but she was not alive in any meaningful sense.

Evelyn's mother sat mute and dazed, unable, or unwilling to walk.

"What's wrong with her?" Evelyn asked Adelaide.

"Shellshock."

A snort. "That's ridiculous. How can she be shell-shocked? She's never seen combat."

Adelaide took a deep breath, reminding herself that Evelyn's retort wasn't really directed at her.

"She has the symptoms; I don't know what else to say."

Evelyn grasped her mother's hand gently, raising it up to her own lips and placing a kiss on the knuckle before letting go. Mary's hand hung suspended in mid-air, not moving from where Evelyn had placed it. Adelaide stared for a moment in bemused horror before Evelyn took hold of Mary's hand and placed it back on the chair's armrest.

She wasn't the only one unnerved by Mary; despite Evelyn's coxing, Riley refused to come anywhere near them.

"The influenza could have damaged her mind somehow."

Adelaide considered how best to tell her that she highly doubted Mary had ever had the flu, that it was most likely a lie concocted to protect Evelyn from her mother's mental break.

Adelaide watched as Evelyn twisted the ring on her right hand, chewing at her bottom lip as she did so. Adelaide reached out, gently brushed her thumb across her lips.

"You'll make it bleed."

Evelyn didn't respond. This was so typical of her, to try and act as though nothing bothered her until the anxiety and anger that bubbled beneath came spilling forth.

"I can't begin to imagine what you're feeling, but please talk to me."

Evelyn remained reticent. Adelaide reached out again, this time taking a hand into her own.

"Evelyn—" Adelaide couldn't finish her thought as Evelyn marched past her out of the room.

Adelaide followed as Evelyn, full of righteous fury, marched towards her father's office. Even with her greater height, she had difficulty keeping pace, such was Evelyn's determination to confront her father.

Not a single sound had passed Evelyn's lips since leaving her mother's side. It reminded Adelaide of the day she had first set eyes upon her; a resoluteness born of a need for truth. No one had been there for Evelyn that day, but Adelaide was here now, and she would not let her barrel in without being prepared for what she might hear. She caught Evelyn's wrist, spinning her around to face her.

"Stop and think for a moment," Adelaide said.

"What is there to think about?" Evelyn yanked her hand away. "How dare he? How could anyone lie about such a thing? What kind of man tells their daughter that their mother has died?"

"I don't trust McGowen's motivation in telling you this. Why now?"

"Guilt." Evelyn scoffed.

"That woman wouldn't be capable of—"

"I never would have thought my father capable of such vile deceit, but here we are," Evelyn said, gesticulating so wildly that Adelaide had to step back to avoid being struck. "The cave entrance, those marks. The second time you went down there, you said there were less than before. What happens when they're all gone?"

Adelaide considered this for a moment. Had whatever drove Charlie to butcher himself been the same catalyst for Mary's catatonia?

"I'm going to have an answer," Evelyn said, before turning from Adelaide to the door. She hit the study door with her fist once, then, not waiting for an answer, flung the door open.

"You never could have loved her, or me," Evelyn said.

"I did what was best," Bramwell muttered, not looking up from his papers. He didn't ask what Evelyn was so angry about; he knew precisely what she referred to. McGowen must have forewarned him.

"You did what was easy for you." Evelyn's fist slammed against the desk.

Bramwell set his pen aside and rubbed at his temple, a gesture Adelaide had seen Evelyn do a hundred times. "I did it to protect you. If you knew what your mother was ..." Bramwell trailed off.

"If I knew what?" Evelyn demanded.

"Her obsession with the caves ever since she was a little girl. She'd been coming up from the village exploring them for years, even when warned not to. She begged me to build the house here; to incorporate them into the foundations so she could continue to do so. You took so many years to come that I let her play at it—it kept her busy until it was time to be a mother, and I thought she had put it all behind her. Then, you got older and were never home, doing god knows what with whatever floozy crossed your path, and she slipped back."

"You blame me."

142

"She invited evil to this house, but you brought sin here first. Then she invited Elizabeth and Greyson, when they promised her they could help her wield its power."

"Whose power?" Evelyn asked.

"I don't know what dwells in those caves. Your mother told me once that those marks, witch marks she called them, were made over the centuries by those who sought to keep what lurks down in its depths sealed there, unable to enter the world above."

"We've seen the marks," Adelaide said. "Twice. The first time we went there, the marks covered every inch of wall extending at least fifty feet from the mouth. The second time it was considerably less."

"The first time I saw them it had to be at least two hundred," Bramwell said warily.

"What happens when they've all disappeared?" Adelaide asked.

"I've said too much already." Bramwell lifted his hand to cut Adelaide off. "Go."

"You can't ignore whatever's going on here," Evelyn said.

"What's going on here is a load of superstitious nonsense your mother lost her God damn mind over." Bramwell stood in front of Evelyn.

143

There was nothing for it. No matter what they said, it would not sway him. The very notion of something beyond the world he knew was unfathomable to him. Regardless of what evidence they placed before him.

"Go," he intoned, once again.

Adelaide dragged Evelyn away.

ᚠᚦ

That same night, Adelaide and Evelyn sat in Evelyn's bedroom, discussing what to do next. They had talked about bringing in a doctor, someone outside of Ashthorne's realm of influence. This was quickly dismissed, though.

Evelyn's mother could easily be hidden away. With the rest of the household denying her continued existence, they would dismiss Adelaide and Evelyn as loons. All anyone had to do was walk to the churchyard and see a stone—much brighter than many others, yet quickly succumbing to the weather—that bore Mary Ashthorne's name. The only other option was to smuggle her out.

CHAPTER SEVENTEEN

They returned to where Evelyn's mother was, to find she was no longer there. Adelaide's first instinct was to check if the car was still there. It was.

"She must still be here, in the house."

Evelyn chewed at her bottom lip.

"Evelyn it's okay. We'll find her."

"It was to be expected I suppose," Evelyn said. "It was nothing but a tease to get me to stay. Marry me off to Edwards, where I'll be no trouble."

"Your father is having doubts. With a little pushing, we could convince him to be rid of Edwards for good, McGowen too."

"He may have doubts, but when it comes to it, he is a spineless, feckless excuse of a man." Evelyn picked up the rocking chair, slamming it against the wall. "I won't leave without her, but believe me, we will be leaving."

145

Adelaide took Evelyn in her arms until her sobs subsided.

ᚠᛈ

They scoured the house, finding locked door after locked door. Mary's silence made it impossible to know which, if any, she could be behind. Mrs Lennox following them didn't help, with her cloddish footsteps and heavy breathing.

"Let's stop for now," Adelaide whispered. "We're not getting anywhere." She raised her voice. "Perhaps Mrs Lennox would be so kind as to make some tea?"

"I don't have to listen to you."

Evelyn stormed off towards her bedroom. "Just make the fucking tea," she called out.

ᚠᛈ

Reverend Peters came that afternoon.

Adelaide and Evelyn were in the sunroom, Adelaide having quit her role as nurse to be able to spend every moment with Evelyn. It was safer for them both never to be

146

alone in a house where it was so easy to hide someone. Despite Evelyn's request for her to let it go, she continued to gently admonish Evelyn for never exploring the house as a child, remaining oblivious to all its hidden rooms and secrets.

"How could you have never noticed a cave beneath your house?" Adelaide was asking, as both the Reverend and Mr Ashthorne walked into the room. Evelyn's eyes flashed in anger. She made to stand up, but Adelaide's hand settled on her thigh, preventing her from rising.

"Reverend. What brings you to visit today?" Adelaide smiled; a genuine smile born from knowing that this man was not a threat to her, but merely an annoyance to overcome.

Edward smiled back, teeth bared in a vicious parody of amicability.

"Miss Frost, I've come to see Miss Ashthorne. Though it is always a pleasure to be in your company, I'd like to speak with her alone."

"No. Anything you wish to discuss can be said openly," Evelyn said.

"Evelyn, don't be so disrespectful," Bramwell said.

"It's quite alright, Bramwell. I was hoping to come to an arrangement that would be satisfactory to all concerned."

Without saying it directly, Edward was offering Evelyn a chance to have her mother back, in exchange for her co-operation. Adelaide clenched her jaw. Evelyn glanced at her, knowing that now it was her turn to keep Adelaide from doing something she'd regret. She put a hand on her shoulder.

"What are you proposing?" Evelyn asked.

Edward scoffed, "I am indeed proposing, Miss Ashthorne."

"And supposing I refuse?"

"You of course have every right to, although this would be a wonderful opportunity to forge familial bonds which would otherwise be denied if you were to continue on your—um—current course."

Bramwell stared at his feet, unable to look at Evelyn as Edward threatened her entire world.

Adelaide wanted to tell Evelyn to cut her losses; that her mother would never regain her sense. That surely her mother would never want her married by force to such a vile man.

But how could she? She had no doubt that deep down, Evelyn knew the woman who had sat rocking vacantly in that chair was no longer her mother and never would be. But what if there was a chance, however small, that she could recover? Adelaide couldn't deny her that prospect.

"I'll leave," she said, getting up. Evelyn's hand fell from her.

"We'll speak later," Evelyn whispered. Now it was Adelaide who couldn't bear to look at her, as she left the room.

ᚠᛈ

Kettle in hand, Adelaide was dismayed to see the fire on the stove had gone out. She desperately needed a cup of tea after the day she'd had; she even briefly considered running out to use the gas stove Evelyn kept in the conservatory, thinking it would no doubt be quicker than trying to rekindle the fire.

But the wind was whipping icy drops of rain with the kind of velocity that makes them sting when they strike your face.

She set the kettle down upon the stovetop, grabbed a few small logs from the bucket beside the stove, and opened the door.

As she placed the wood, a glint of light caught her eye.

There was something reflective in there. She reached in and pulled it out.

Adelaide studied the object, a piece of polished wood, and though it was charred and smashed, she recognised it as the puzzle.

ᚠᚦ

"Why didn't you come to bed last night?" Evelyn hugged Adelaide to her. Adelaide gently pushed her away.

"I didn't think it was appropriate."

"Appropriate?"

"If you are to be married." Adelaide tried to keep her tone even. Whatever decision Evelyn came to had to be hers alone. Adelaide would never be able to live with herself, should she force Evelyn to choose between being with her or her mother's safety.

"Don't act as if this is a betrayal."

"How is it not?" Regret immediately flooded in. Any attempt to be unbiased in this was doomed to failure. Adelaide moved closer to her, eyes locking on Evelyn's, her tone softer now. "But it's a necessary one. To do otherwise would be to betray your mother."

"Adelaide, I'm not marrying him, I never could. But I have to play his game. Until the three of us leave together."

"Do you have any idea how moronic that sounds? Your mother, wherever she may be, cannot walk out of this house. And I'm afraid if we stay much longer, nether will we. McGowen told you about your mother to keep you in this house, to keep you in this village so that you'd marry Edward. It seems every corner I turn the pair of them are there, whispering, plotting."

"You've not listened to me at all. I know it's all a trap. But I won't be caught in it."

"Promise me?"

"Promise you what?"

"That you won't be trapped forever."

"I promise."

ᚠᚦ

That same morning, McGowen revealed where Evelyn's mother had been hidden, saying that she was free to see her.

"Maybe it's best if you stay here," Evelyn had said to Adelaide.

Adelaide sat alone. The caves beneath the house were the key to all of it. Bramwell himself had said Mary was the one obsessed with these caves. That she had invited people into the house. It seemed Evelyn had forgotten all of this.

An unwillingness to believe Mary had orchestrated her own fate. Adelaide had to find out what was in that cave, and she would have to do it alone.

CHAPTER EIGHTEEN

Armed with an army issue Efanden torch, Adelaide stood at the top of the steps leading into the cave. She had dressed for the expedition in a pair of trousers she had liberated from Charlie's trunk. Adelaide wiped her palm against her thigh. Despite the dimpled oilskin of the torch body, it felt as if it could slip from her grasp, clattering down into the unknown. The blood roaring in her ears, Adelaide started the descent into the below.

ᚴ

Adelaide's shoulders convulsed involuntarily. The cave was not overly cold, and Adelaide had dressed warmly, yet dread gripped her heart in an icy dam clasp. Soon, the steps levelled out to the plateau where she and Evelyn had first seen the witch marks. Common sense told her to turn back, but Adelaide knew that to free Evelyn from the house she would have to push past the marks and their protection, to the inky blackness where lord knows what resided. There was a scurrying sound. Rats, she told herself, but even rats would avoid this place.

Adelaide called out. Her "Hello" bounced around the rock walls. What had she expected?

An answer?

Yet there was an undeniable presence in that darkness: Adelaide felt it, the same way she knew Evelyn had slipped into bed when her mind was clouded by sleep and her eyes hampered by the pitch of night.

She directed the beam towards the mirror; as her eyes adjusted, she saw only herself. Eyes wide with fear, hair wild. She let out a bark of laughter.

How had she come to this? Hunting for monsters in the dark, long-dead mothers found sequestered in secret rooms? She wiped a tear away.

"Fuck me."

A cat's hiss answered. At least it sounded like a cat's hiss, but had she really heard it? She had felt it reverberate inside her head.

"It's not real!" She screamed the words, trying to drown out the noise; how could she, though? When it was inside her, penetrating her mind?

The hiss was joined by a cacophony of low, guttural growls, hisses, and screeches. Animalistic, primal sounds which Adelaide had no frame of reference for. Behind them was a formation of vowel sounds.

A language. As she stood frozen, the jumble of sound formed into cohesive words. It was then she turned and ran.

Once Adelaide reached the safety of the top of the steps, she vomited. Her stomach muscles continued contracting painfully, long after her stomach was empty. She crawled on hands and knees, away from the mess she had created. She laid on the floor, the marble mercifully cool on her forehead, until the nausea subsided. Then she closed her eyes, and drifted into oblivion.

CHAPTER NINETEEN

Adelaide opened her eyes, and for one horrible moment, thought she was back in the cave. As she came round, she realised the ground beneath her was too soft, warm fur nuzzled her hand, and a familiar shaft of moonlight fell across her face.

"Thank god you're awake." Evelyn's hand cupped her cheek, her thumb gently caressing her. Embarrassment gripped Adelaide that Evelyn had seen her in such a state.

"I'm sorry," she sobbed.

"Shh, it's alright." Evelyn crawled onto the bed and put her arm around Adelaide, drawing her to her breast. "What happened? I've never been more scared in my life than when I found you. I thought you were dead."

"If we don't leave this house, we will be. "

Adelaide scrambled away from Evelyn's arms, so she was sitting up.

"I know what it wants, what she wants. This thing beneath your house—your home—has been watching you all your life. There's been a plan and you loving me, any woman, isn't a part of it."

"I don't understand what you're saying."

"That your purpose is to make babies, to ease her way into this world. With a ready-made army, each child harbouring a piece of her," Adelaide babbled, unable to keep the words from leaving from her lips, yet fully aware of how insane she sounded.

"How have you found this out?"

"I heard it—but I didn't—it was in my head. A jumble of pictures and sounds, but somehow they came together, and I understood."

Evelyn leapt from the bed, Riley following her, circling around her feet.

"We leave now."

"But your mother?"

"I believe what you're saying is true, and I can only think she knew. That for my entire life, she planned to sacrifice me to that thing. That it was my only purpose for ever being in this world: to churn out young like a sow on a farm."

Adelaide couldn't bear for Evelyn to think this way, to think that all the love she had known from her mother was a lie.

"Why would she be so accepting of you preferring women? Maybe she was glad because it meant you could escape that fate," Adelaide protested weakly.

"Oh Adelaide, I know what you're doing, and I adore that, but I don't think that's true." Evelyn wiped a tear from her eye. "Why haven't you moved? I mean it. We go tonight."

ᚠᚦ

Evelyn had not unpacked since the last time, so once Adelaide had changed into fresh clothes, they were on their way. Even though it was drawing near to two in the morning, the front hall was packed with Edward's twisted congregation.

What are they doing here? Adelaide thought. She'd calmed down somewhat since they'd decided to leave, had put her theory of being watched by the mirrors to the back of her mind. It'd been ridiculous to have ever thought of it in the first place.

Yet here they were, and standing front and centre were McGowen and Edward. Now they stood next to one another, Adelaide could see the family resemblance. In fact, how could she have been so stupid as to not have seen it before?

"I swear the pair of you will never learn," McGowen sneered. "Running away again."

Evelyn moved forward, squaring up to McGowen.

"We are leaving, and nothing you can say can convince me otherwise."

"Oh, the time for talking has long passed. Your mother had such high hopes for you: even when you turned out to be defective, she still thought we could put you to use. It is a shame you can't impregnate a woman yourself. A whore such as you would have given us a dozen brats by now."

Evelyn's hand cut McGowen's words off, making contact with her face with enough force to fill the room with a resounding crack. McGowen reeled from the blow, whilst Edward's face was one of amusement. Catching sight of him, McGowen glowered at Edward, who promptly rearranged his expression to that of anger directed towards Evelyn.

"I'm telling you. Step aside," Evelyn said, her chest rapidly rising and falling.

"You can't keep us here."

"You're my wife. You're not leaving me," Edward said.

"What? No, the engagement is off. I was crazy for ever agreeing to it."

"A much higher power than you promised you to me."

"My father? Well, you can tell him to fuck off!" Evelyn grabbed Adelaide's hand, holding tight. "I don't mind telling him that myself. In fact, why don't you all fuck off out of his house?"

"It's not his house, hasn't been for a long time. Business in ruins, he signed over the property and in return we paid his debtors, saved his livelihood. He asked that you not be told," McGowen scoffed. "However, now that he is no longer with us, we don't have to honour that part of the agreement."

Edward smirked as Evelyn took another step forward, only for Adelaide to grab a handful of her coat, pulling her back. Adelaide saw the tears building in Evelyn's eyes.

"What have you done with him? Where is he?" Adelaide said, placing herself between Evelyn and the crowd.

"He's dead," Edward stifled a yawn. "It's late, and I'm bored." He placed a hand on Adelaide's chest. "So, why don't you take her upstairs until we decide what to do with you?"

Riley, during all this, stood barking and baring his teeth at all who threatened his mistress. Out of the corner of her eye, Adelaide saw McGowen step towards him, drawing her leg back to administer a kick. Moving faster than she had ever done, she pushed McGowen, causing her to fall back into the throng. Evelyn quickly scooped Riley up.

Surrounded, they had no choice but to retreat upstairs.

CHAPTER TWENTY

"Cover the mirror," Adelaide said, as soon as they were in Evelyn's room.

"What's wrong?"

"Cover the mirror!"

"You don't have to shout," Evelyn said, taking a shawl and throwing it over it. "Why are you so panicky?"

"It's mirrors, it's always been the mirrors. I've been so fucking stupid!" Adelaide stopped pacing. "The window. It's anything glass—anything reflective."

Evelyn drew the curtains, then went to take Adelaide in her arms.

Using a darning needle, Adelaide carved one of the symbols she'd seen in the cave into the mother-of-pearl blade. She didn't know if it would do any good; Charlie's good luck trinket hadn't done him any good in the end. But had it done any harm? Adelaide didn't think so. She'd chosen three overlapping circles reminiscent of a Venn diagram, and as she looked upon her work, she felt a sense of calm wash over her. Riley trotted over.

"What do you think?" she held the blade in front of him, his reaction, as with most things he encountered, was to lick it.

"Yeah, we won't be having that," she said, as she withdraw the blade from him. "But I'm glad it has your approval."

ᚠᚦ

Time ticked by. Adelaide and Evelyn alternately dozed, unable to reach the full crest of sleep. The curtains were drawn, but the bright sunlight of noon poured through the gaps. There was a click of the door. McGowen entered, closing it behind her.

Evelyn scrambled up, determined to finish what she had started with that first slap. Now that McGowen was alone,

Adelaide felt no compulsion to hold her back. While Evelyn manhandled McGowen into the chair, Adelaide pushed the dresser in front of the door, barricading it. Having successfully prevented any hope of rescue for McGowen, Adelaide thought of drawing the knife that she now kept in her boot. It wasn't sharp, but it might serve to scare her. She decided against this, though, and went to join Evelyn, who stood in front of a nonplussed-looking McGowen.

"You girls do have spirit."

"Are you here to gloat?" Evelyn bent to McGowen's level, staring into her unblinking eyes.

"I'm here to tell you exactly what I expect of you. Do you think it's a coincidence that the flu affected not one person in this village? That people from all over the country come to visit, to spend money in our tearoom, buy trinkets from our shops? She gives that to us, protects us, allows us to thrive."

"Thrive? The men of this village were sent to die in foreign lands. Where was she then?" Adelaide said.

"Which is why she needs to be at full strength. Other wars will come. We must be prepared."

"This all comes down to Roskopf?" Evelyn said.

"You've always been right that he is nothing but a charlatan. A man who has no idea what he's doing. That's what

164

made him so easy to manipulate. He genuinely thinks he is helping. And he is, just not in the way he expected." McGowen yawned. "He's of no consequence now. He, and the soldiers in his care, have fulfilled their purpose, they gave her strength. The blood spilled so far is that of outsiders, although we will do anything necessary to protect the whole. Hence your father." McGowen's face contorted itself into its best approximation of remorse.

"Why Charlie?" Adelaide said, her voice a whisper. "What had Charlie done to deserve what happened to him?"

"Does anyone really deserve anything that happens to them?" McGowen sneered. "Adelaide, you had plenty of warnings. That night in the hall, the horse. Yet you still wouldn't leave. I had to do what I did to Charlie."

Adelaide's head pounded, an incessant pain behind her eyes, and before she knew what she was doing, she was holding the blade to McGowen, its tip digging into the soft flesh beneath her jaw.

It may not have been sharp enough to slice, but it would certainly pierce.

The woman just laughed in Adelaide's face. "They all know I'm here. If I don't come back, they'll come up here and—well, there's no telling what they might do to you. Or Evelyn."

Adelaide backed away. Still shaking with rage, she replaced the knife into her boot.

"Nobody expects you to live as man and wife with Edward, no matter what he says," McGowen said, addressing Evelyn. "Just fulfil one wifely duty. You and Adelaide would be free to live your life together. You don't have to raise the children. There are many in the village that will give them homes. You can be both matriarch and saviour of the community."

"If it's that bloody wonderful, why don't you do it?" Evelyn tightened her grip on the other woman's wrist.

McGowen laughed. "She's fixated on you; after all you would have been her vessel for rebirth had you not come two months early whilst your mother was away from the house."

"That's the criteria? To be born in the house?" Adelaide narrowed her eyes at McGowen. The woman obviously believed what she was saying; the danger they faced right now lay with her and Edward's fanatics, people who would do anything to keep Evelyn in this house.

"The house is a shell placed over a nest. Anywhere on the grounds would be enough."

"What about the village? What influence does she have there?"

"Enough to protect it. Evelyn, we would prefer it to be you that has the honour of bearing a child for her. But it doesn't have to be you. It's not set in stone. We will discard you," McGowen nodded towards the barricade. "And if you think that is going to stop anyone from charging through that door. Well ..."

"Let Adelaide go, you've no use for her."

Adelaide opened her mouth to protest, but McGowen answered.

"Nonsense. She makes you happy, plus do you think we'd allow her back into the world armed with the knowledge she has? And a determination to rescue you?"

"She won't say a word," Evelyn said.

"Our offer is a generous one. She wishes for you to be happy. So, she stays with you, or she dies." McGowen grinned, and it was then Adelaide noticed the mahogany spot on her cheek.

When had that appeared?

"If you're tired of this whore, we can get you another."

Evelyn looked at McGowen for a moment before moving to the door and pushing the dresser aside

"Get out."

McGowen stood, rubbing her wrists and hands. Her nail beds had turned purple, though there was no possible way

Evelyn could have held her wrists tightly enough to cut off the flow of blood.

"Feel free to make use of the house." A choking cough caused her to double over for a minute before she regained her composure. "We want you to feel at home, after all."

ᚠᛈ

True to her word, McGowen did not interfere with Adelaide and Evelyn roaming the house. Evelyn had insisted that they go to the sunroom at the rear of the house; there was something comforting about being able to see the grounds knowing that the conservatory was just beyond the tree line, she said. Evelyn spent hours sitting across from her mother, silently watching, appraising. Adelaide stood leaning against the doorway, observing Evelyn.

She watched her, knowing that Evelyn wanted to scream, shout, ask her why. But knowing that it would do no good. Days dragged on; confined to the house, time and routine were lost. They used sleep to pass the time, regardless of the hour. Edward had disappeared from the house, but there always remained enough of his followers to ensure there was no chance of escape for them.

168

CHAPTER TWENTY-ONE

Once again, Evelyn sat watching Mary, whilst Adelaide stood watching Evelyn. Riley still refused to come anywhere near Mary, preferring to stay safely ensconced in Evelyn's bed.

"Do you think she understands?" Evelyn asked.

Adelaide, startled from her reverie, blinked uncomprehendingly. They had been in silence for so long that Adelaide's mind had drifted. Evelyn left her mother's side. She cupped Adelaide's cheek. "Never mind. Do you understand what's going on right now?" Evelyn whispered, her hand moving downwards and back to gently entwine in Adelaide's hair.

"Sorry, I don't know where I drifted off to," she said, leaning into Evelyn's touch. "To be honest, no, I don't think she does. That thing almost ripped my mind apart. It succeeded with your mother."

The sound of heavy footfall was rapidly advancing.

"McGowen is on the warpath again, judging by that clomping," Adelaide laughed. "Wonder what she's got to say for herself today?"

The joke quickly turned sour, however, as Edward, flanked by two men; healthy, young, not from the village, appeared at the doorway.

"Still snivelling around her, I see." Pointing his chin towards Mary, he addressed Evelyn, ignoring Adelaide entirely. "She as good as sold you, you can't fight it much longer."

"I know what Elizabeth told you, but I want you to know, I expect you to be compliant." He motioned to the two men who each took Adelaide by an arm, forcing her into the chair. They had come prepared, producing leather straps from their pockets. They secured her arms to the heavy oak chair, ignoring her legs.

Thank God, Adelaide thought, as they would have surely seen the knife in her boot.

One of the men handed Edward a small piece of wood with leather attached to each end: a gag. He walked over, towering over Adelaide. Even now, Adelaide couldn't help but taunt him. He balled his fist, striking her; she felt a tooth give way, breaking off into a jagged piece. She tried to spit it out, but Edward clamped his hand over her jaw, forcing her mouth shut.

Evelyn started forward, only to be captured by Edward's men.

"I'm going to enjoy making you watch," he said, as he forced the gag into her mouth. "You can leave now," he barked. The men left the room as Edward once again advanced on Evelyn.

He pressed Evelyn up against the wall. "This is my reward." His free hand swept through the air. "The business, the wealth, the prestige. I don't give a fuck about you. Truth be told, Adelaide's much more my type." Evelyn's eyes widened in horror as Adelaide fought against her restraints.

Edward laughed. "Don't worry about her. she's safe for now. You, on the other hand …" He ran his hand up Evelyn's side. "I won't enjoy this, but you might. After all, you've never had a man. I can't imagine what she could possibly do to you that a real man couldn't do better."

Mary stared blankly ahead; her eyes flashed with the barest flicker of understanding.

Get up, help her! Adelaide willed Mary. Adelaide thrashed against the leather straps; her jaw ached from biting down on the wooden gag.

It was getting harder and harder to breathe. The broken tooth had lodged itself under her tongue, the sharp edge piercing into flesh. Blood mixing with saliva threatened to overwhelm her. Fear gripped hold, as she realised she was about to choke to death on blood and spit whilst helplessly watching the woman she loved being violated. Blinking back the water in her eyes, Adelaide saw a slight movement of Mary's fingers.

She forced herself to calm down, to focus on Mary. The woman wasn't a complete statue; Adelaide had seen slight movements of hands, feet, and head before. Movement again: this time the shoulder lifted. Was she breaching through whatever thrall this entity had her under? The Blue John-handled knife was in Adelaide's boot. She tried to show this to Mary by thrusting her right leg out, hoping she'd see the handle protruding from the leather.

"Why don't we move to somewhere more comfortable?" Edward said to Evelyn. "Or do you think she'd like to watch?" He threw her to the floor. "I think this time she can watch. Adelaide, take notes. You may learn something new."

He loomed over Evelyn. He didn't see that Mary had risen behind him, the heavy crystal vase gripped firmly in both hands. She brought it down on his head. Adelaide thought it may shatter, but there was only a dull thud. Mary still held the vase in her hands.

The crystal glittered like rubies.

Mary stood, bewildered by what she had done. Evelyn scrambled up from the floor.

"Mum?"

Mary turned to look at Evelyn. Her mouth opened and closed wordlessly.

"It's going to be alright. You saved me." She went to hug her, but realised that the vase Mary still held in front of her served as an encumbrance. Evelyn took the vase, gently placing it back on the table. Evelyn glanced at the crimson smears on her hands, then wiped them on her skirt. She embraced Mary, whose arms hung limply at her side. Her fingers twitched, grasping at thin air. Adelaide, unable to wait any longer, tapped her boots.

"Oh God." Evelyn rushed to her, unbuckling the leather strap that held the wooden peg in her mouth. "I'm so sorry."

The gag gone, Adelaide turned her head to the side, spitting out the blood and saliva mix, the tooth emitting the faintest clatter as it hit the hardwood floor. Evelyn gently touched her jaw.

"I'm fine—" She winced as Evelyn gingerly probed her. "Just get me out of this bloody thing."

Evelyn quickly undid the wrist restraints. Adelaide got up on unsteady feet.

"Is he dead?" Adelaide looked down at Edward.

"I don't know," Evelyn answered.

Adelaide knelt. There seemed far more blood than a person could stand to lose, pooling around his head, but still there was a slight rise and fall of his chest, almost imperceptible, but steady.

"We should go." Adelaide drew the knife from her boot, before standing back up. She grabbed Evelyn's hand. "I won't let them hurt you again."

"Hurt me? I'm not the one with a missing tooth. I'm so sorry, we should have left weeks ago."

"Can she walk?" Adelaide said, indicating Mary.

Evelyn took Mary's hand and tugged; she took a few tottering steps forward.

"You both stay behind me."

"We need to get Riley." Evelyn said.

They moved through the eerily quiet house, Mary at an excruciatingly slow pace.

"Where have they gone?" Evelyn asked.

"Who knows, but I imagine McGowen is holding court over them." The sound of metal on stone emanated from the bowels of the house. Adelaide held a hand up, indicating for them to stop.

"What are they doing?"

"Witch marks."

Adelaide and Evelyn stared at Mary. Her voice creaked from a year of non-use, but with the returning presence of mind came the return of the beauty she had bestowed upon her daughter. Adelaide could clearly see how Evelyn would look in thirty years' time.

"The witch marks?" Evelyn gently took her mother's hands in both her own, encouraging her to go on.

"We've been erasing them for years. It's not as easy as you'd think. You are working against the faith of the person who originally carved it. Each strike of the hammer and chisel requires a tremendous amount of mental strength. It took me years of work to remove even a fraction of the marks. How many followers have they?"

"Thirty or so."

Adelaide thought back to that day in the church. "I'd say closer to forty." Her tone was flat as the weight of the knowledge pressed on her. All of them working together, erasing the boundary that kept the force in check. The same realisation must have been had by Evelyn.

"We can't let them finish," she said, her face flushed with determination. Regaining her mother had revitalised the fight in her.

"The likes of us against forty of them isn't going to end with us victorious," Adelaide said. All she wanted was to get Evelyn out of this damn house.

"If all the marks are erased, what happens then?" Evelyn asked, ignoring her.

"It will be easier for her to take hold of a body, what else I don't know," Mary said blankly.

She knows, Adelaide thought, *she knows, and she'll lie about not knowing to win Evelyn back.*

"All the more reason for you not to be here. No, you. No baby. No end of times," Adelaide snapped. "You've even got your mother back to boot. No more excuses, Evelyn."

Evelyn hesitated, before nodding her agreement. Adelaide moved on, footsteps echoing on the hard floor. The sound was only her own though; she turned to see Evelyn and Mary had stopped.

"We stay," Mary said, her grip tight on Evelyn. "Once I've had time to talk to you and explain what a great honour it is, you'll be happy to abide. We'll even find you a better man, a gentler man." Mary stroked Evelyn's hair with her free hand whilst she spoke.

"I'm never going to submit to this." Evelyn tried to break away from Mary, but her mother held her fast.

Adelaide grabbed the arm encircling Evelyn and pulled. No effect. Mary's arm was a rod of iron, muscles taut with an unnatural strength running through them.

"Come on," Adelaide urged.

"I can't believe the time is so close. I've waited all my life, and now I can feel her power growing. I didn't lie when I said I don't know exactly what will happen. But I do know that it will be glorious. Adelaide, you can be a mother too. My beautiful girl and her wife. Mothers to a new and better world."

Evelyn and Adelaide continued to struggle.

"Evelyn," Mary cooed. "Can't you feel the power! It belongs to you, it's been waiting for you your entire life. I failed her when I gave birth to you so far from home. You can rectify my mistake. When you understand, you will be honoured to lie with a man, of your own choosing, and fulfil the destiny that should have been mine.

"Evelyn, you've been spoilt; never knowing hunger or desperation. Your father thought he'd saved me when he built this house for me. No, he saved us all. Will save us all."

Mary turned to address Adelaide.

"Evelyn was always destined to be a queen, you could do so much worse than being her consort. I know your life hasn't been as blessed as my daughter's. Your family discarded you so easily, didn't they? You loved your brother dearly, but you know deep down that he would have done the same upon finding out what you are, had he lived—"

"How do you know this?"

"You've spoken about this, to Evelyn, late at night with your friend Charlie—"

"Don't you dare say his name," Adelaide said, her jaw clenched so tightly that it came out as a hiss.

"I'm truly sorry about Charlie. You're a part of my family now, and I'd never want for you or Evelyn to suffer."

The woman was truly unhinged if she couldn't see that she was causing Evelyn to suffer that very moment. There was no other option; taking the knife, Adelaide slashed at Mary's forearm. Evelyn's eyes flashed in horror.

Mary didn't flinch as the blood ran down her front. Adelaide froze, uncertain as to what to do next. For Evelyn's sake, she didn't want to seriously hurt Mary; had thought that a shallow swipe would force her to let go of Evelyn.

"Let go." Adelaide tried again to pry Mary's arm from Evelyn. Mary batted at her, sending her careening across the floor, hitting the heavy oak door. The knife flew from her hand and clattered to the floor. Evelyn clawed and hit at her mother as she was dragged towards the mouth of the cave.

WILL YATES

⟨HAPTER TWENTY-TWO⟩

Adelaide awoke dazed. Every part of her ached, as the entire floor beneath her seemed to hum. The vibrations cut to her very core. She must have been out for some time, as the light blazed through the glass leaves of the door, carpeting the hall with colour. Adelaide got unsteadily to her feet.

Had it always been this bright?

She took a few steps forward, her equilibrium regained. She looked across the autumnal forest floor until she found that flash of deep purple and gold.

She picked up the knife and went to face Mary and McGowen.

As Adelaide made her way to the cave mouth, the sound of metal against stone ebbed and waned until finally coming to a full stop. Had they finished erasing the witch marks, or were they taking a rest from their work? McGowen and Mary were deep in conversation at the top of the steps; an unconscious Evelyn lay on the floor. McGowen looked deeply unwell, a blueish tinge upon her lips as she spoke.

"We are very close to finishing, although many of them are complaining of fatigue."

"They can push through it," Mary said, before looking wearily towards Adelaide. "What now?"

What now, indeed?

There she stood, battered and bruised. What had she expected? If she couldn't hurt Mary, maybe she could take McGowen down with her instead? That would be an immensely satisfying end. Mary came toward her.

"Let Evelyn come with me," Adelaide raised the blade toward Mary, hands shaking, "and I won't hurt you."

Mary pressed the knife down with her palm.

"I can see why Evelyn loves you so." She brushed Adelaide's hair back from her brow with maternal tenderness. "When she wakes, I'll tell her you left without her." She enveloped Adelaide in a hug. "Shh, it will be painless. I wish it needn't be this way, but you've proven to me you will never give up on Evelyn." She let Adelaide go, taking a step back from her. "And frankly, it's too exhausting a prospect."

Adelaide braced for an attack, when a miracle struck. McGowen, who had been watching impassively, turned a deeper shade of blue and kneeled over. Her mouth opened and closed silently as she gasped for air. As McGowen hit the ground, a series of screams erupted from the cave, followed by a scrambling of bodies spewing forth from the dark depths. Adelaide guessed the people rushing by totalled to twenty or so. How many were still down there?

It was clear what had struck down McGowen and those still in the tunnel: influenza, the same thing Edward had promised to protect the village from. Adelaide had witnessed the ferocity with which it struck down its victims, the way it razed through whole families. From first cough to coffin in a matter of days, but this was far beyond anything she had seen before.

"Crisis of faith."

"What?" Mary snapped.

"The faith they had in your goddess has faltered. You all promised them a life free from war and plague. Now they are being struck down. I'd say that's enough for anyone to have second thoughts." Adelaide laughed. "Your friend made it clear that she feeds on pain and suffering. Did you really think that'd she give a fuck about the people in this village? If she's free, what's to stop her doing whatever she likes? She knew they feared sickness, and she gave it to them in abundance."

"They are unworthy, and the work is nearly done. I need no one else now but Evelyn."

"Don't you love her?" Adelaide's knuckles turned white. The knife felt hot and heavy in her hand.

"I do. This is the best thing that could happen to her, even if she doesn't realise it yet. She won't have the life I did; she'll have power, she will rule as queen of this world." A sickly violet glow crept from the depths of the cave. "She's almost here, almost free from her confinement."

The violet light grew stronger.

"I want that for Evelyn too." Adelaide said.

"You do?" Mary looked at her incredulously.

"The world isn't kind to people like us. Evelyn never wanted to leave her home. To leave you. How is it fair that she loses her inheritance, everything that is her birth right, in exchange for living as herself?" She crept closer to Mary. "I love Evelyn with all my soul. If this is what needs to be, I'll do it. Let me talk to her; explain how we can all be a family here. Together, in this house."

Mary's features softened. "I'd like that."

Feeling bold, Adelaide pressed Mary. "The witch marks? Are they all that have kept her in place all these years?"

"Yes. And now only a few remain." Mary's features brightened. "We can erase them together. Our first act together as mother and daughter."

Adelaide nodded in faux affirmation. Mary had been so desperate to believe Adelaide would agree with her that all sense had once again left her. "You said before that it takes a tremendous force of will to remove them?"

"You have to overcome the faith of those before."

"Is it the belief or the symbol that matters?"

"I believe the symbols used are completely arbitrary. It's the power the person puts behind it." Mary extended her hand to Adelaide and led her down the steps.

‹HAPTER TWENTY-THREE

The light cast the corpses that littered the cave a deep purple.

Only, not all the bodies were strictly corpses. It was better to think of them that way. Better to ignore the gasping breaths, the blooded faces, the demented cries. Even if she had the desire, there was nothing Adelaide could do to help.

Mary stopped to pry hammer and chisel from a man's hand. He fought to keep it, but was no match for Mary.

The last witch mark was the largest and deepest. A pattern of linked circles a foot wide, it was the one Adelaide had chosen to reproduce in miniature on her blade.

Mary tried to push the tools into Adelaide's free hand. "I don't know if I have the strength."

"You'll find it."

Mary entreated once more for Adelaide to take the tools, but Adelaide shook her head. Sighing, Mary turned to the

185

mark. Setting the chisel to the stone, she raised the hammer and struck a blow. Adelaide wouldn't have thought it possible for the stone wall to be made smooth by a single stroke. The tools weren't important, merely an extension. The knife crackled with static, sparks of blue igniting from its tip.

The lilac glow was encroaching further, lighting up even the darkest edges of the cave. The noise roaring in her head, along with a growing pressure in her sinuses that normally heralded the coming of a thunderstorm, combined to make a pain which Adelaide had no basis of comparison for. The carving upon the blade seemed to glow faintly and, despite all she had witnessed and experienced, struck Adelaide as being utterly absurd, making her wonder if this was all a horrible dream.

Some might call it cowardly to stab a woman in the back. But Adelaide saw no other choice: the mark was almost gone. She plunged the knife into Mary's left shoulder, forcing her to drop the chisel. Adelaide held tight to the knife's hilt as Mary swung round. The hammer missed her head by inches. Unwilling to lose her weapon, Adelaide yanked the knife out of Mary, losing her balance and falling backwards into the violet haze. She watched as the silhouetted form of

Mary plucked the chisel from the ground and, with one last strike, removed all that remained of the witch mark.

ᚠᚦ

The flash of light scorched Adelaide's eyes. A sudden drop in temperature caused her to cry out in pain from the frigid mineral in her hand, the ache reverberating up her forearm.

Thick, dark tendrils crept across the floor, converging into a hideous parody of a human form. Mary's self-proclaimed Goddess towered over her; Mary dropped to her knees, her face twisted into rapturous wonder.

The thing—Adelaide could think of no other possible way to describe it—stood sixteen feet tall, dwarfing Mary.

Mary may have been right in her assertion that this was female, but it was a vicious, twisted, exaggerated version of femininity. Pendulous breasts swung in front of the creature, lactating some viscous spitting liquid on the stone floor.

Its stomach was swollen, an overripe fruit ready for the skin to split and burst. Most disturbing of all was the glistening slit between knurled legs.

It reached out with one colossal hand to pet Mary on the head; the appendage engulfed Mary's skull; the hand bobbed gently three times before it withdrew. It seemed to regard Mary with a wry amusement, as befitted a creature as ancient and eminent as itself. It was clear to see why the people who had known of the thing's existence had carved their marks again and again into the rock. As the creature shuffled past, it turned to face Adelaide, fixing glowing violet eyes on her. It seemed to smile, features contorting to show teeth. It turned away to continue its amble towards the stone steps.

Towards Evelyn.

Adelaide saw with crystal clarity what she needed to do.

ᚠᚦ

Adelaide scrambled to her feet, hoping to God that the speed with which the creature moved was its limit and that it was not just taking its time. She sprinted past the creature. She was fast, but not quite fast enough: with one sweep of its long limb, it caught Adelaide's ankle. She tripped forward but kept her momentum going. Something heavy hit the small of her back. She let out a yowl of pain, but kept going.

She made it to the steps. She didn't have long, and doubted that the knife would prove sharp enough.

No! If she believed it was sharp enough to score stone, then it would be. School lessons came half-remembered to the surface.

She made the first stroke. Relief flooded through her as it cut deep. She went to make her second stroke, when something yanked at her ankle. Her chest hit the floor as her supporting arm gave way beneath her. Mary tugged at her again, pulling her away from the carving.

Adelaide kicked out; felt her boot connect with Mary's jaw, who reeled from the force of the blow. Scrambling forward again, Adelaide found her place and continued carving.

The creature was seconds away. Adelaide finished. Would it be enough, though? She climbed over the step, placing the carving between her and it. On unsteady legs, Adelaide stood, the height gained by being on the steps raising her to an even keel with the creature. It stared at Adelaide, but would not shift closer. It was Adelaide's turn to smile now, as the thing's gaze went from the Æ carved into the step, back to Adelaide, them back to the Æ.

"Fuck you," she muttered.

ᚠ᛬

The creature stood a moment more, then poked Mary with its foot. Adelaide's eyes widened as Mary stirred. How could she have been so stupid as to forget about Mary?

No worry, she only had to defend the mark from Mary. How hard could it be? She was only human, after all.

Mary sat up groggily as the creature was gesturing towards the step. Mary nodded in understanding. Adelaide braced herself as Mary looted another body for tools. Mary stared at the sigil Adelaide had carved.

"What made you think of that?" Mary delicately traced its lines as she spoke.

"It was the obvious choice."

"The ligature, A and E together. Your first thought was to put you and Evelyn together."

"It always will be my first thought."

"What a coincidence. That in the old English it means ash," Mary said absently.

"You've no intention of letting that thing back out, have you?" Adelaide asked.

Mary smiled.

"Cross the line," Adelaide pleaded.

"I can't."

"Of course, you can. If you don't do it now—"

"If I leave now, it will always wheedle at my mind, waiting for a way back in. So that it can get out."

"We won't let you. We'll go as far away from this place as is necessary."

Mary slowly stepped back from the line.

"Tell Evelyn I am sorry." Mary turned, raising the chisel up, dropping the hammer; she didn't need it.

Mary slashed at the thing's grossly distended stomach. Æ shone wetly on the creature. It let out a shriek, lashing out at Mary with one long limb. There was a snap, then Mary hit the floor, unmoving. It was too late, though. Mary had inflicted the damage. It continued its unearthly screeching, flailing limbs which, as it moved, dissolved into liquid smoke, globules wetting the floor, hissing and spitting like fat sizzling in a hot pan, before seeming to evaporate and disappear. The violet light flashed dizzyingly on and off as the creature was in its death throes, until finally it went dark, and the screaming ceased.

ᚠᚦ

Adelaide dragged aching limbs up the steps. Her chest constricting, head arching, back to the safety of Evelyn, who still lay on the floor, a perfect point of comely calm amongst the carnage. Adelaide knelt beside her. Cupping her face, she gently stroked her thumb across the curve of her cheek. Evelyn shifted slightly, her hand coming up to gently grasp Adelaide's hand.

"Tickles." Evelyn slowly sat up. "Jesus Christ!" Evelyn stared at McGowen's body, which had turned a bleak grey.

"There appears to have been an outbreak," Adelaide wheezed.

"Where's my mum? Is she alright?" Evelyn scrambled to her feet as Adelaide tried to follow, only getting halfway up before collapsing.

"Adelaide?"

She couldn't breathe. Desperation clawed at her. She had to tell Evelyn that at the very end, when it mattered, Mary had done the right thing for them all. For Evelyn.

Adelaide was aware of Evelyn carrying her to her bed. Aware of Evelyn tending to her, speaking in soft sooth-ing tones as she mopped her brow. Cleaned her. Several times, Adelaide talked to Evelyn about what had happened down there. Every time Evelyn told her to shush, to save her energy. Adelaide felt certain she was on the precipice of death, felt many times that she would gladly step off that ledge, if it meant her suffering would end.

Eventually, it did.

EPILOGUE

It was a month before Adelaide was well enough to travel, a month which Evelyn had spent in the abject terror that Edward would return. A fear that proved unfounded. McGowen and her brother were proven to be liars. Bramwell had never sold the house to them, which explained Edward's determination to marry Evelyn.

"I can't stay after all that's happened here," she'd said, as she told Adelaide of her ideas for their future together. Her plan was to sell the house and travel.

"What about that thing?" Adelaide asked.

"From what you've told me, it's dead. I'll arrange for the entrance to be blocked. But why should we have to stay and be custodians of this house?"

True to her word, tradesmen came in, first erasing the cave's entrance and then the door.

"Will you miss it here?" Adelaide asked, as they stood for the last time in the hall. Adelaide knew she would miss the play of colour on Evelyn's pale hair.

"No," Evelyn said bluntly. "I've never spent that much time here. My parents are gone. Truth be told, I'd have gone back to Manchester and stayed if you hadn't caught my attention."

"Even though you were such a bitch to me at first?" Adelaide teased.

"You'll always hold that against me. Won't you?"

"Maybe, maybe not." Adelaide took Evelyn into her arms, running her fingers through her hair before taking her lips with her own. Riley circled around their feet, eager to leave.

"Although it might be for the best if we just focused on the good that came from our time here," she said, breaking away from Evelyn and picking up her luggage with one hand whilst offering Evelyn the other.

Evelyn took it with a smile.

"Agreed."

ACKNOWLEDGEMENTS

First of all I'd like to say thank you to the indie horror community, never before have I met such an awesome and supportive bunch.

And a few extra special thank yous to the following awesome people.

Andrew M Roberts for encouraging me to pick up the PEN again and get it done when a massive chunk of the manuscript disappeared into the digital ether weeks before the submission deadline.

Nat Edwards and Shauna McEleney for being there when I needed them and not blocking me when I messaged at what was, quite frankly, ungodly hours.

Donnie Kirchner for his absolutely stunning artwork.

And Antonia Rachel Ward, EIC of Ghost Orchid Press and all round lovely person, for taking a chance on this story and supporting me, and so many others, in their writing and publishing journey.

And thanks to you, reading this right now, for sticking with this book to the end. I hope you were entertained, and if you happen to be one of those people who reads this stuff first (no judgement) please turn to chapter one now.

April Yates

May 2022

ABOUT THE AUTHOR

APRIL YATES is an author of sapphic horror and Gothic fiction, based in Derbyshire, UK.

Her short stories have appeared in *A Quaint and Curious Volume of Gothic Tales* by Brigid's Gate Press, and *Blood & Bone: An Anthology of Body Horror by Women* by Ghost Orchid Press, amongst others.

The phrase "Beautifully smooth with a zesty tang" appears here because she read it on a jar of lemon curd at 2a.m. and made an ill-advised quip that she was going to steal that for her bio, which tells you all you really need to know.

You can keep up to date with publications at aprilyates.com or find her spouting nonsense on Twitter @April_Yates_

ALSO AVAILABLE FROM GHOST ORCHID PRESS

GHOSTORCHIDPRESS.COM